This book belongs to:

....

CONTENTS

STORIES BY IAN ROBINSON
ILLUSTRATED BY JOHN HARROLD
STORY COLOURING BY GINA HART
© Express Newspapers 2003

John Harrold.

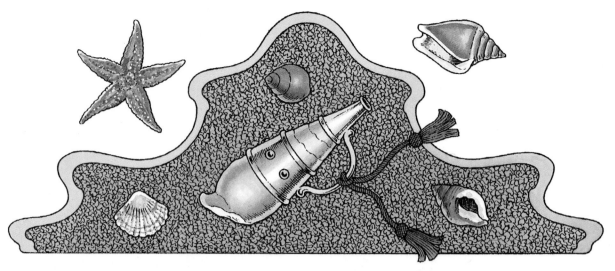

RUPERT

John Harrold.

The DAILY EXPRESS Annual

Published by Pedigree Books Limited
Beech Hill House, Walnut Gardens, Exeter, Devon, EX4 4DG
email: books@pedigreegroup.co.uk

No 68

£7.50
RU68

RUPERT and

*Rupert and Bill decide that they
Will go out walking for the day…*

It is a sunny morning, at the start of the holidays and Rupert and Bill have decided to go on a long hike… "Let's try somewhere different!" says Bill. "How about heading for the Lake?" "Good idea!" agrees Rupert. "If we take the path through the woods it will be even more of an adventure." The pair continue until they reach the edge of the trees. "Straight ahead!" says Bill. "All we have to do is keep on going in the same direction…"

the Water Bottle

"This way!" says Rupert. Bill agrees,
"The map showed a path through the trees."

"Look, Rupert! There's a hollow tree!"
"A hideaway! Let's go and see..."

As Rupert and Bill follow the path through the woods, they spot a hollow, old tree. "Look at that!" calls Bill. "It's like Robin Hood's hideaway! I'm sure I could climb inside." To his delight, Rupert's chum finds that the tree is even bigger than it looked. "We'll both be able to fit in here!" he cries. "Come on, Rupert! Let's see if it's dry. It will be just the place for a secret camp. I'll mark it on the map, so we can be sure of finding it again."

"There's lots of room. I'm sure that you
Will fit inside the tree trunk too..."

RUPERT'S PAL MAKES A DISCOVERY

"These leaves feel like a bed! I mean,
They're springy, like a trampoline!"

"Then, suddenly, to Bill's dismay,
He feels the leafy floor give way…"

Bill tumbles through an old trap door
And lands with a bump on the floor…

He clambers up and looks around -
Astonished at what he has found.

Inside the tree, Bill finds a mass of dry leaves, which have been blown in by the wind. "It's like a huge nest!" he calls. "I wonder how long all these have been piling up? They feel soft and springy, like a mattress…" Jumping up and down on the leaves, Bill suddenly feels the floor start to give way. "Help!" he cries. Rupert leans forward to grab his chum's arm, but it is too late. With a despairing wail, Bill sinks down through the leaves and disappears from sight…

To Bill's amazement, he falls down through the leaves into an underground chamber. Clambering to his feet, he peers around in the gloom. "It's a secret room!" he gasps. "There must have been a hidden trap-door…" The underground chamber is full of odd-looking bottles and jars. There are candles too and a heavy metal cauldron. Everything Bill sees is dusty and covered in cobwebs. "Rupert!" he calls. "Wait till you see what we've found. I think it's some sort of hide-out!"

Rupert and the Water Bottle

RUPERT EXPLORES THE HIDE-OUT

"Rupert!" cries Bill. "Come down and see -
We've made a great discovery!"

"It's someone's hide-out! What a find!
Let's look at what they've left behind..."

"Whose are these books and ancient charts?"
"A wizard, versed in magic arts..."

"This bottle's full! It might just be
A magic potion! Shall we see?"

"Are you all right?" asks Rupert as his chum reappears. "Never felt better!" smiles Bill. "Come and have a look! There are stones, set in the wall, you can climb down, like steps..." "What a find!" blinks Rupert. "If the trap-door hadn't given way, we'd never have known it was here." "That's right!" nods Bill. "Whoever built this certainly meant to keep it well-hidden. Funny place to make a home, isn't it? Judging by all the cobwebs, I don't think it's been used for years..."

As the two chums start exploring the secret chamber they can hardly believe the things they find... "There are books and charts," says Rupert. "Flasks and bottles too!" says Bill. "I think it's some old wizard's lair!" "You might be right!" agrees Rupert. "We'd better not touch anything, in case he comes back." "There's no harm in just looking," says Bill. Picking up a glass bottle, he suddenly notices that it is still full. "Magic potion!" he cries excitedly. "I wonder what it does?"

9

RUPERT SEES A MAGIC BOTTLE

*"Be careful Bill! You might just find
The stuff's a poison of some kind…"*

*"Don't worry! I'll just pour a drop
To make a spell and then we'll stop…"*

*"That's odd, Rupert! You saw me pour
The bottle out, but now there's more…"*

*"It's like a magic trick - somehow
The water's back inside it now…"*

Bill is so excited by his find that he carries the bottle out of the secret room and removes its silver stopper… "Be careful!" warns Rupert. "It could be poisonous, for all you know." "Don't worry," says Bill. "I'll only tip some on the grass. Wouldn't it be fun if it really was a magic potion? I know, let's try making a spell as well. Oh, potion show what you can do, please turn the grass from green to blue…" "Not that much!" gasps Rupert. "You've nearly emptied the bottle!"

Bill stops pouring and looks at the liquid in the bottle. "I've hardly used a drop!" he says. "In fact, I'm sure the level hasn't fallen at all…" "You're right!" blinks Rupert. "But that's impossible! I saw you tip out the whole lot. Look at the wet patch on the ground. It took more than a drop to do that!" "How odd!" says Bill. "It must be a trick bottle. Not as good as a magic potion but still quite a find! Perhaps we ought to take it back to show to Tigerlily's father…"

RUPERT TAKES COVER

The two chums hear a rustling sound
Which makes them start and turn around...

"There's someone there! Quick, follow me!
We'll try to hide behind a tree!"

The pals take cover. "This should do -
We'll see who else is coming too..."

"Look!" Rupert laughs. "All we could hear
Were just the footsteps of a deer!"

The two friends are still marvelling at the magic bottle when they suddenly hear a rustling sound from the bushes nearby. "W...what's that?" blinks Bill. "I think there's somebody coming!" whispers Rupert. "It might be the chamber's owner!" gasps his chum. "Quick, Rupert! We'd better hide." Dropping the bottle, the pair run off through the woods as fast as they can. "Take cover!" gasps Rupert. "We'll hide behind a stand of trees, then wait to see who's there..."

Turning off the forest path, the two chums plunge through the undergrowth then hide behind a tall tree, waiting to see who is coming... For a long time, all they can hear is the chirping of birds. Then, Bill hears the bushes stir again. "They're there!" he hisses. "Creeping up on us, from the sound of it! Perhaps they saw me go in?" Rupert peers out anxiously, then suddenly starts to laugh. "It's a deer!" he chuckles. "That's what we could hear! Fancy running away..."

RUPERT FINDS THE WAY

The chums have wandered off the track
And don't know which way to get back…

"There's only one way we can see!
I'll climb to the top of a tree…"

"The Professor's tower! Now I know
Exactly where we need to go…"

The pals spot Bodkin. "Hey!" they cry.
"We've found a hide-out, just nearby…"

Relieved that their fears were unfounded, Rupert and Bill head back through the forest towards the hollow tree. "We must be nearly there now," calls Bill. "I can't see it anywhere!" says Rupert. "In fact, I'm not even sure we're on the right path!" "You mean we're lost?" blinks his chum. "I'm afraid so!" nods Rupert. "We must have taken a wrong turn…" Searching all round, he finally decides to climb to the top of a tree and look for familiar landmarks. "All we need is a pointer in the right direction…"

Climbing to the top of the tree, Rupert gazes out over a leafy canopy to the very edge of the woods. "I can see the Professor's tower from here!" he calls excitedly to Bill. "We're not that far away. I know which direction it's in now, so we won't get lost again…" Sure enough, the pals soon reach the far side of the forest where the distinctive building can be seen across the fields. "There's Bodkin!" says Rupert. "Let's go and tell him what we've discovered…"

RUPERT TALKS TO BODKIN

*"I've never heard of it before!
Perhaps the Professor knows more…"*

*"He's gone away for days, but when
He gets back home, I'll tell him then…"*

*Next morning, Bill is keen to look
Again. "I know the path we took…"*

*"There's Farmer Brown! I wonder where
He's taking all those sheep up there?"*

When Bodkin hears the pals' story, he shakes his head. "You find all sorts of things in those woods!" he says. "It's one of the oldest parts of the forest. The Professor might know something about it, but I'm afraid he's away at the moment. Won't be back for days…" Giving the chums a drink of lemonade, he waves goodbye as the pair set off along the path home. "Sorry I can't be more helpful," he smiles. "An underground hide-out's quite a find. It's probably been there for years and years…"

Next morning, Bill calls at Rupert's house to suggest going back to the woods to look for the chamber again. "I've been thinking about whose hide-out it was!" he says. "A hermit, perhaps? Living there, all alone…" "Or an outlaw!" says Rupert. "Someone like Robin Hood. On the run from the King's men…" The two pals are still on their way to the forest when they see Farmer Brown, driving a flock of sheep. "He's moving them out of the lower field," says Bill. "I wonder why?"

*"The low field's flooded! It's too deep
For cows to stay, never mind sheep!"*

*"A proper flood, and no mistake!
The river's spread out, like a lake!"*

*The pals walk on, along the "shore"
Then head into the woods once more...*

*"We need to find the hollow tree!
The trouble is, it's hard to see..."*

Farmer Brown explains that he is having to move his sheep because the lower fields are all flooded. "The river must have burst its banks!" he says. "I don't know how, exactly. I didn't hear it rain in the night and everything was fine down there yesterday." "It looks like a pond!" says Bill. "Two fields completely submerged!" nods the farmer. "I've never known anything like it! Lucky I came by when I did or all the sheep would have had to swim to safety..."

Leaving the farmer to tend his flock, Rupert and Bill go down to the flooded fields to take a closer look. "It's funny the river should suddenly flood, like that!" says Rupert. "I suppose it must have worn away the bank." The pair continue on their way, towards the woods where they found the secret chamber. "It was somewhere near here, I'm sure!" says Bill. "The hollow tree is what we need to find. I can't remember the exact direction, but I think we came this way..."

RUPERT SEES THE FLOOD SPREAD

No matter how they search, the pair
Can't find the hide-out anywhere…

"The water's rising!" Rupert thinks.
"The flood has got much worse!" he blinks.

In Nutwood, Growler has a plan
To stop the water, if he can…

"This flood's something I can't explain!
We haven't had a drop of rain…"

No matter how hard Rupert and Bill search the forest, they still can't see the hollow tree… "Perhaps it's magic!" shrugs Bill. "That might explain why no-one has found the hidden chamber before." "Perhaps," says Rupert. "But I think it's more likely we're just looking in the wrong place." Eventually, the pals decide to give up and go home. On the way back, they see that the flooding from the river has got even worse. "Goodness!" blinks Rupert. "The water-level's rising fast!"

As the two pals reach the outskirts of Nutwood, they are surprised to find P.C. Growler preparing a thick wall of sandbags. "Can't be too careful!" he says. "If the water-level keeps on rising at this rate, the whole village could be flooded…" "It's happened before!" nods Gaffer Jarge. "I was a nipper at the time. It had been raining for ages then, though. Not like today. I can't understand it. Rivers don't just go flooding without any cause. 'Taint natural!"

*"The newspaper says that there might
Be further flooding in the night…"*

*"This old barometer of mine
Says that the forecast's dry and fine!"*

*Next day, the sun is shining bright -
"The old barometer was right!"*

*But, looking out, Rupert sees how
The whole of Nutwood's flooded now…*

When Rupert arrives home he finds his parents are also worrying about the flooding… "The newspaper says it might reach the village tomorrow!" says Mrs. Bear. "There's a picture of Gaffer Jarge with a piece of seaweed. He claims it can predict the weather." "I'd rather trust my barometer!" laughs Mr. Bear. As Rupert goes to bed that night he checks the dial for a final reading. "High pressure! Sunny and dry!" he announces. "No danger of flooding then. We can all sleep safely…"

Next day, Rupert wakes to a bright, sunny morning. "Dad's barometer was right!" he smiles. "No rain today…" When he peers out of the window, he can hardly believe his eyes. "The whole garden's flooded!" he blinks. All Rupert can see is the very tops of the trees. "The water's even reached the downstairs windows!" he gasps. "We're cut off, like an island. I wonder what will happen next? If the flooding gets any worse, we'll have to climb on to the roof and wait to be rescued!"

RUPERT IS RESCUED BY HIS CHUM

"It's terrible!" says Mr. Bear.
"The flooding has spread everywhere!"

"Ahoy, there!" Bill calls. "I thought you
Might like to go exploring too…"

"Be careful, Rupert. Try to find
Dry land, if any's left behind…"

"The magic bottle that I dropped
Will pour out water till it's stopped!"

Rupert's parents are astonished by the flooding too. "It's extraordinary!" says Mr. Bear. "The whole village is under water. I've telephoned P.C. Growler and he's trying to get a motor launch from Nutchester to come and collect us all." Just then, Rupert hears a familiar voice calling his name. "It's Bill!" he cries. "He's got a rubber dingy…" "Ahoy, there!" calls Rupert's chum. "I found this in our attic. It's from a trip to the seaside. Not very big, I'm afraid. But I think there's room for two…"

Rupert clambers out of the window and joins his chum in the dingy. "Do be careful!" calls Mrs. Bear. "Don't worry!" says Bill. "We'll head for high ground and look for help there…" As they row away from the stranded cottage, Bill reaches into his pocket and takes out a small, silver stopper. "I think I know what might have caused all this!" he says. "It must be that strange bottle we found and I dropped. If it really is magic, it might go on emptying out more and more water forever!"

RUPERT AND BILL LOOK FOR HELP

"The Old Professor! Perhaps he
Is back by now? Let's go and see…"

Bodkin is safe but can't say when
His master will return again…

"There's one more person we might try -
His hilltop castle's quite nearby…"

"The Wise Old Goat! Let's ask him now -
We've got to stop the flood somehow…"

Who can the chums ask for help? "The Professor!" says Rupert. "Let's go and see if he's back…" When the pair reach the Professor's tower, they find it surrounded by water, like a castle moat. "Isn't this terrible?" calls Bodkin. "The Professor's laboratory hasn't been flooded yet but the water's still rising!" "When do you expect him back?" calls Bill. "Next week, I think." says Bodkin. "He's gone to the South Seas to look at shells. I can't get in touch, I'm afraid. It's too far away…"

As the pals leave the Professor's tower they spot a little island in the distance. "It's the Wise Old Goat's castle!" says Rupert. "He must have been cut off too." The pair decide to ask the Goat's advice. "He might know something about stopping spells," says Bill. "He often makes charms and potions from herbs and wild berries." "It's worth a try," says Rupert. "I hope he's at home." "We'll soon find out," says Bill as they approach the castle. "I can't see anyone from here…"

RUPERT SEES THE WISE OLD GOAT

The two chums pull their boat ashore
Then climb up to the castle door...

They ask the Goat, "Please help us halt
The Nutwood flood. It's all our fault..."

"Remarkable!" the Wise Goat cries.
"That stopper's one I recognise!"

"I've seen it in an ancient book
On alchemy. Let's have a look..."

Landing on the little island, Rupert and Bill clamber to the top of the hill where the Wise Old Goat's castle stands. Ringing the bell, they wait for the door to open... "Rupert!" cries the castle's owner. "How nice to see you. I've been thinking about Nutwood all morning. Terrible flooding from what I can gather..." "That's right!" says Rupert. "We've come to ask your help." "To stop the water from rising any further?" asks the Goat. "That all depends on how it started..."

"Gracious me!" exclaims the Goat as the chums tell him the story of how they came across a secret chamber in the woods. "And that's the stopper from the magic bottle you found?" he asks. "It looks strangely familiar. From a drawing, I think..." Going to the bookcase, he reaches down a heavy, leather-bound volume. "Experiments in Alchemy!" he announces. "Written by one of my ancestors. I'm sure there's something about a flask with a silver stopper in here..."

RUPERT LEARNS ABOUT THE BOTTLE

*"Identical! The flask you found
Was a drought bottle, I'll be bound…"*

*"The magic only ceases when
The stopper's back in place again…"*

*The Wise Old Goat soon has a plan
To help the two chums, if he can…*

*"We need to reach the place where you
First found the bottle. That should do…"*

"That's it!" gasps Bill as the Wise Old Goat leaves through the pages of a book. "A drought bottle!" nods the Goat. "One of my ancestor's finest inventions. It was his old workshop you tumbled into, no doubt. The bottle was meant to be a source of water in times of emergency. Harmless when stoppered but otherwise releasing unlimited quantities. Powerful magic's at work here, I fear. Unless we replace the stopper soon the whole of Nutwood will be completely submerged!"

"We must retrieve the bottle!" declares the Wise Old Goat. Taking a strange box from his desk, he also produces a butterfly net and several lengths of pole. "Launch your dingy!" he calls to Bill. "I'll sit at one end, while you and Rupert row…" Directing the pals back towards Nutwood, the Old Goat tells them to aim for the woods where they first found the hollow oak. "The treetops are still visible," he says. "The bottle must be underwater, somewhere down below…"

RUPERT GOES FISHING

"The viewing box light's glowing red!
That means we're now right overhead…"

"Rupert! Start lowering the net.
Reach down as far as you can get…"

"I see the bottle! Nearly there…"
The two chums hear the Goat declare.

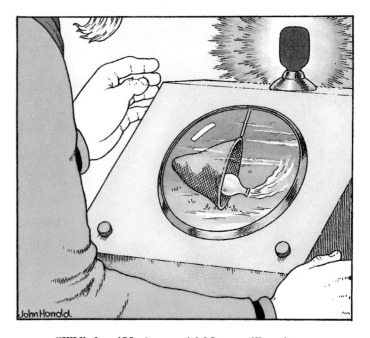

"Well done! You've got it! Now we'll see!
Bring up the net, please, carefully…"

When they reach the submerged wood, the Wise Old Goat tells Rupert and Bill to stop rowing and sit perfectly still. Pressing a button on the strange box, he lets the boat drift until a large red light begins to flash. "We're directly overhead!" he declares. "The viewing box has found the bottle, all we have to do now is catch it…" Handing Rupert the net, he tells him to lower it slowly over the side, extending the handle length by length, until he reaches the bottom of the lake…

As Bill and Rupert lower the net, the Wise Old Goat carefully watches a circular screen on the front of his box… "That's it!" he calls. "You're getting closer and closer. I can see the bottle perfectly clearly now." A moment later, the net itself appears on the screen, gliding slowly through the water towards the bottle. "Left a little!" calls the goat. "Now to the right. Well done, lads. You've got it! Bring the net up gently and we'll be able to have a good look at what we've caught…"

RUPERT FINDS THE MAGIC BOTTLE

*"We've done it! Bravo!" both chums shout
As Rupert lifts the bottle out.*

*"Quick, put the cork in! That's the way!
You've stopped the water now! Hurray!"*

*"The flood's still here, but I think we
Can rectify that magically..."*

*"Wait here!" the Goat says. "While I look
At spells in my ancestor's book..."*

When Rupert and Bill lift the net from the water they can see the magic bottle, still gushing water like an open tap... "Bravo!" calls the Wise Old Goat as the pair land their catch. "Now, Bill, get ready to stop it with the cork!" Lifting the bottle from the net, Rupert holds it steady while his chum pushes back the silver stopper. "That should do the trick!" says the Goat. "Now we have to find a way to get rid of all the flood water so that Nutwood gradually returns to normal..."

Although Rupert and Bill are glad to have stopped water pouring from the magic bottle, they are still mystified as to how the Wise Old Goat plans to clear up Nutwood's flood... "It's like a huge lake!" says Bill as they row back to the castle. "There's nowhere for the water to go..." "You'll see!" laughs the Goat. "My ancestor's invention caused all this. I think he can help us put things right as well. You two wait there, while I go inside and fetch his book of spells..."

RUPERT HELPS TO CAST A SPELL

"I thought I saw a counter-charm!
It should soon clear up any harm…"

"Reverse the spell and help restore
All Nutwood as it was before…"

A gentle wind begins to blow
Then, gradually, it starts to grow…

"A hurricane! We'd better hide!
Quick, everybody. Get inside!"

The Wise Old Goat emerges from the castle with his ancestor's book and a long, wooden staff. "I thought so!" he smiles. "We can reverse the spell with a counter-charm. Rupert, you keep the bottle safe, while Bill holds the book…" Reading aloud from the spell to cure droughts, the Goat strikes the ground with his staff and recites another rhyme. "Reverse the spell and take away the flood you caused, without delay. Let Nutwood's fields appear once more and all be as it was before…"

As he finishes speaking, the Wise Old Goat stands still as a statue, staring out intently across the flooded fields. At first, nothing seems to happen. Then a wind starts to ruffle the surface of the water, blowing stronger and stronger. The sky grows dark and a huge, swirling cloud appears… "It's a tornado!" cries Bill. "You're right!" calls the Goat. "We'd better take shelter inside. It's only just starting. I think we're going to be right in the eye of the storm…"

RUPERT SEES A WHIRLWIND

As the whirlwind spins far and near
The flood begins to disappear...

It moves towards the castle, where
It spins, like a top, in mid-air.

The Goat tells Rupert he must hold
The bottle ready when he's told...

"Remove the cork and wait until
The whirlwind gets here. Just keep still..."

From inside the Old Goat's castle, Rupert and Bill watch the whirlwind swirl and spin over the countryside around Nutwood. "It's sucking up water!" cries Rupert. "Reversing the spell!" nods the Wise Old Goat. "You can see the cloud above growing fuller and fuller..." As the waters clear, the tornado wheels towards the castle, like a giant spinning top. "Up the stairs to the top of the round tower!" calls the Goat. "And don't forget to bring the bottle..."

As they reach the top of the tower, the chums can see the whirlwind approaching... "It's coming straight at us!" blinks Bill. "Exactly!" says the Goat. "We're in just the right place..." Telling Rupert to take the stopper from the bottle, he gets him to hold it out at arm's length. "Keep it steady and don't move!" he calls. "You'll be perfectly safe, so long as you do exactly as I say!" Removing the cork, Rupert stands ready and waits for the cyclone to arrive...

Rupert and the Water Bottle

RUPERT ENDS THE STORM

The whirlwind stops where Rupert stands
Then follows the Wise Goat's commands…

"It's nearly gone! The end's in sight!
Quick, Rupert! Put the cork in tight…"

"Well done, the bottle's full once more
And Nutwood's as it was before…"

"I'm glad the flood has gone but, still,
It was quite fun as well," says Bill.

The sound of the wind grows louder and louder. As Rupert holds the bottle out, the whole swirling mass sinks down in the sky until it is only inches away from his outstretched arm. "The time for Nutwood's flood has ceased!" commands the Wise Old Goat. "Draw back the water you released…" To Rupert's amazement, the tail of the whirlwind sinks into the bottle, like a huge genie returning to its lamp. "Nearly done!" laughs the Goat. "Now get ready with the cork…"

As the last of the whirlwind vanishes inside the bottle, Rupert pushes home the stopper with a cry of triumph. "Well done, you two!" says the Wise Old Goat. "We won't be troubled by that again!" Taking the bottle from Rupert, he puts it safely away in a cupboard while the chums have a well-earned snack. "What an adventure!" says Rupert. "Magic!" laughs Bill. "Although I think it will be quite a while before I try climbing inside any more hollow trees…"

25

*One morning Rupert takes a track
Across the fields towards Sam's shack…*

The holidays are over and Rupert and his chums have started a new term at school. Dr. Chimp has asked them to write about famous explorers and Rupert thinks he knows just the person to ask for help… "Hello!" cries Sailor Sam as he opens the door to his shack. "Come in and I'll see what I can find. Explorers and navigators are what I like reading about best of all. It's fun to try to trace their journeys on a map…"

26

and the Ringer

He's come to ask about the ways
Explorers sailed in olden days...

"Columbus, Magellan and Cook,
I'll show you the main routes they took..."

"Who do you want to know about?" asks Sam. "Christopher Columbus is the most famous navigator, I suppose, then there's Magellan, da Gama, Captain Cook..." "Columbus!" says Rupert. "We learnt a rhyme about the year he set sail." "I know that too!" laughs Sam. "In fourteen hundred and..." Before he can finish, the pair hear a faint ringing sound. "It's my bell!" says the sailor. "There must be someone at the door..."

"A bell!" says Sam. "Outside, I'm sure.
There must be someone at the door."

RUPERT LEARNS OF A THEFT

*"There's no-one here! The bell's gone too -
Somebody's taken it, but who?"*

*"The Fox brothers! I might have guessed!
Those two pranksters are such a pest..."*

*The Foxes blink in shocked alarm -
"It wasn't us! We've done no harm!"*

*"Not you?" glares Sam. "That's very well!
But somebody's stolen my bell!"*

Sam opens the door and gives a cry of surprise. "The bell's gone!" he gasps. "It's disappeared..." "How strange!" says Rupert. "It was here just a moment ago. I rang it when I arrived." "Somebody must have taken it!" says Sam. "That explains the noise we heard. Fancy stealing my old ship's bell!" "Who would do such a thing?" asks Rupert. "Freddy and Ferdy Fox!" says Sam as he looks out across the common. Following his gaze Rupert spots the twins, running away from the shack...

"Not so fast!" calls Sam. "I want a word with you!" "Us?" blinks Freddy. "We're on our way to school." "Past my cabin!" says Sam. "You didn't just stop outside?" "No!" says Ferdy. "We're late! We've had to run all the way from home." "You mean you didn't take my bell?" asks Sam. "No!" says Ferdy. "What made you think that?" "It's vanished!" explains the sailor. "Nothing to do with us!" says Freddy. "We sometimes ring doorbells then run away but we wouldn't steal one like yours..."

28

RUPERT ARRIVES AT SCHOOL

"We're late for school!" the Foxes call.
"Now Dr. Chimp will scold us all…"

The pals arrive. "No-one's gone in!"
"We're still all waiting to begin…"

At last, the teacher comes to say
That school is starting for the day…

"I'm sorry to be late, you see
I don't know where the bell can be…"

Leaving Sam's shack, Rupert and the Fox twins hurry along the path to school… "We'll be late now!" says Freddy. "Fancy thinking we'd stopped to take his bell! I didn't even have time for a second piece of toast…" To the friends' surprise, the playground is still full when they finally arrive. "What's happened?" asks Rupert. "Why hasn't everyone gone in? It must be ten past nine…" "No sign of Dr. Chimp!" says Gregory. "We're still all waiting for him to come out and ring the bell!"

As Rupert and his pals wait in the playground their teacher eventually appears with a whistle, which he blows as loud as he can… "Good morning, everyone!" calls Dr. Chimp. "I'm sorry about the late start but I've been searching high and low for the school bell! I'm sure I saw it earlier today but now it seems to have vanished!" "Magic!" cries Bill. "Nothing to do with me!" says Tigerlily. "I'm looking forward to school today. I've made a map of Marco Polo's travels…"

RUPERT MEETS FARMER BROWN

When school ends, Rupert points out how
Two bells have vanished strangely now…

"There's Farmer Brown! It seems to me
He's lost something. What can it be?"

The anxious farmer tells the pair
He can't find his sheep anywhere…

The pals walk on until they hear
A sheep bell ring. "They must be near!"

When school finishes, Rupert walks home across the fields with Gregory… "I wonder who took Dr. Chimp's bell?" asks the guinea-pig. "Probably Freddy and Ferdy…" "It wasn't them!" says Rupert. "They didn't take Sam's bell either, though he was sure they had at first." "Two missing bells!" says Gregory as he hears what happened at the sailor's shack. "Do you think they're linked?" "Perhaps," says Rupert. "Why, look, there's Farmer Brown. It seems that he's lost something too…"

"Hello!" calls Farmer Brown. "You haven't seen any sheep, have you?" "No," says Rupert. "I've lost a whole flock!" shrugs the farmer. "I'm sure I heard the bell-weather just then but I can't see where she's gone!" "The sheep's leader?" asks Gregory. "That's right!" nods the farmer. "The one with a bell…" "We'll keep a careful look-out!" promises Rupert. The chums continue on their way. "I can't see any sign of sheep," says Gregory. "Me neither!" says Rupert. "But I'm sure I can hear a bell…"

RUPERT FINDS THE LOST SHEEP

"Look!" Gregory cries as he sees
The sheep. "They're in amongst the trees!"

"Come on!" calls Rupert. "We can tell
The way by following the bell…"

"Another bell! Let's go and see
If we can find whose it can be…"

They've found the flock, but Rupert's sure
The bell sounds higher than before…

The chums walk on, towards the distant sound. "Over there!" cries Gregory. "I can see some sheep by the edge of the wood!" "You're right!" blinks Rupert. "They look like stragglers. The rest of the flock must be in amongst the trees. They'll all be following the leader's bell…" By the time the two chums reach the trees, the last of the sheep have disappeared into the wood. "Come on!" calls Rupert. "I can still hear the bell. Let's try to find where they've gone…"

The pair follow a grassy path deep into the forest. "I wonder which way the sheep went?" says Gregory. "I don't know," admits Rupert. "The ringing's stopped now. Perhaps we ought to turn back." The friends have almost given up when they suddenly hear another bell. "It's higher than the first!" says Rupert. "Perhaps it's a different sheep?" The chums soon spot a line of sheep standing by a gap in the trees. "A third bell!" whispers Gregory. "It's even higher than the others…"

RUPERT MEETS A STRANGER

*The two pals stare, amazed to find
A boy with bells of every kind...*

*"That bell is one I recognise -
It came from Sam's shack!" Rupert cries.*

*"Rupert! Look! I've found our school bell -
He must have taken that as well..."*

*"You've stolen bells from everywhere -
Now tell us why!" demand the pair.*

Pushing through the flock of sheep, Rupert and Gregory come to a clearing in the wood. To their amazement, they see a strange boy, sitting on a rock... "It's him who's ringing the bell!" whispers Gregory. "He's got all sorts of them there!" The pals watch fascinated as the boy rings one bell after the other. "He's writing something too!" murmurs Rupert. "Every time he rings a bell." Just then, the pals spot the bell from Sam's cabin. "So it was you!" cries Rupert. "You're the thief..."

At Rupert's words, the boy gives a startled cry and leaps to his feet... "Here's Dr. Chimp's bell too!" says Gregory. "I'd recognise it anywhere!" "A bell snatcher!" gasps Rupert. "I suppose you stole all the others as well! From Farmer Brown's sheep, for one thing. That's why the whole flock followed you here..." "Why did you take our school bell?" asks Gregory. "What do you want it for? We saw you writing something down..." "You did?" says the boy. "Oh, dear!"

RUPERT HEARS ABOUT THE BELLS

"I'm not a thief! Not normally -
I just need lots of bells, you see…"

"I'm making up a tune, that's why,
For bells to play, from low to high…"

"Though Nutchester's not far away
There's nowhere there where I can play!"

"My father's the town-crier! He
Thinks that's what I should want to be…"

"I…I can explain everything!" says the boy. "I'm not a thief. Well, not normally. I know I shouldn't have taken the bells. I promise I'll give them all back when I've finished…" "Finished?" blinks Rupert. "Finished what?" "Composing!" says the boy. "I'm trying to write a tune!" "With bells?" asks Gregory. "That's right!" nods the boy. "That's why I need so many. Small ones for the high notes, big ones for low notes. I write them down as I go…" "So that's what we could hear!" smiles Rupert.

"A composer!" says Gregory. "I've never met one of those before…" "Oh, I'm not really a composer yet," says the boy. "I'd like to be, one day, but my father wants me to stick to just one bell." "Your father?" asks Rupert. "Mr. Jingle!" says the boy. "Nutchester's town-crier! I'm his son, Dingle. He wants me to be a crier too. That's why I've come to Nutwood. To practice my ringing in secret. You won't tell him what I'm up to, will you? He thinks I've gone up into the hills to try out loud cries…"

RUPERT HELPS TO PLAY A TUNE

*"My composition's finished now -
I need to play it through somehow…"*

*"Please take these bells and both join in -
I'll get the score and we'll begin…"*

*"You've two bells each. One low, one high.
I'll count to three and then we'll try…"*

*The two chums follow Dingle, then
Play the whole tune through once again…*

Dingle tells the chums he is writing a tune for a bell-ringing contest in Nutchester. "It's tomorrow!" he says. "I've just finished in time! All I need now is some help to play it through…" "Help?" asks Rupert. "More players," explains the composer. "A team of ringers to perform the piece properly. Two bells each would do the trick. I'll conduct from the score and tell you when to ring…" "It does sound fun!" says Gregory. "You mean you'll help?" asks the boy. "Of course!" smiles Rupert.

The chums are given two bells each as Dingle gets everything ready. "I'll call out when it's your turn to play!" he explains. "You've each got a high bell and a low bell. Rupert low means the school bell. Gregory high is the little cat's bell. I'll count to three, then off we go…" The pals follow Dingle's lead, ringing first one bell and then the other. "Both high bells together to finish!" calls the boy. "That's perfect!" "Bravo!" laughs Rupert. "Now let's play it through again…"

34

RUPERT GOES TO NUTCHESTER

"Tomorrow, will you help me play
In Nutchester? What do you say?"

The pals agree. "I'll see you there!"
Calls Dingle as he leaves the pair.

Next day, the chums are keen to start
And catch the first bus to depart...

In Nutchester the pair can see
A poster. "Look!" calls Gregory.

"That was marvellous!" says Dingle. "If only we could play as a team tomorrow..." "I don't see why not," says Rupert. "Gregory and I can come to Nutchester on the bus. We'll meet you rupere before the competition begins." "Wonderful!" cries Dingle. "I'll wait for you both by the Market Cross. I'll need to keep the bells overnight, but I promise to give them all back the moment the contest ends." "Till tomorrow, then!" says Rupert. "We'll set off as soon as we've finished breakfast..."

Next morning, Rupert and Gregory catch an early bus from Nutwood to Nutchester. "Sorry I'm late!" puffs the guinea-pig. "I forgot to set my alarm clock!" Travelling along country lanes, past farmsteads and fields, the pair look round excitedly as they reach the outskirts of the market town. "There's a poster!" calls Gregory. "And quite a crowd of sightseers," says Rupert. "Nutchester's even busier than normal. It looks as though everyone is on their way to the competition."

RUPERT MEETS HIS NEW FRIEND

Just by the Market Cross, the pair
See Dingle - who's been waiting there...

"Hello!" he smiles. "Well done, you two.
I knew I could rely on you..."

"Oyez!" calls Mr. Jingle. "In
A moment our show will begin..."

"Professor Stave is here to test
The ringers and decide who's best."

Stepping into the crowded street, the pals soon spot Dingle, who has been waiting for them by the Market Cross. "Hello!" he calls. "Isn't this a marvellous turn-out? I hope you're not nervous about playing in front of so many people?" "No!" smiles Rupert. "I'm just looking forward to hearing all the other ringers..." "There are some very good teams," says Dingle. "Though I don't think many will be playing new tunes. That's where we'll have an advantage over everyone else..."

Leading the way from the Market Cross to a bandstand in the park, Dingle shows the chums where the ringers are to perform. "That's my father!" he says, pointing to the stage. As he speaks the town-crier rings his bell to make an announcement. "Oyez! Oyez! Nutchester's bell-ringing festival is about to begin. All teams are invited. Professor Stave will award prizes for the best tunes and tintinnabulation! Last year's champions will open the ringing - Popton's Pride..."

RUPERT HEARS THE BELL-RINGERS

The Popton ringers start to play -
It seems they're sure to win the day...

A school team's next. They're good as well -
But who will win? No-one can tell...

"Is that the last team? Are you sure?
What's this? It seems that there's one more..."

"A late entry!" calls Gregory.
"Bravo! Let's see who they can be..."

The Popton champions take the stage to a round of loud applause. At a nod from their leader, they pick up their bells and start to play. "Wonderful!" says Dingle. "Same tune as last year, but I suppose that's what they know best..." The next team are a lot younger and come from one of Nutchester's schools. "St. Cecilia's!" calls Mr. Jingle. "First year in the contest, I think. Ringers of the future..." "Not bad!" whispers Dingle. "They got a bit muddled towards the end. Our turn's coming soon!"

The bell-ringing contest continues, with several teams from nearby villages taking the stage. At last Mr. Jingle declares that there seem to be no more contenders. "Just one!" calls a voice from the audience. "What's this?" blinks Dingle's father. "A late entry?" "That's right, sir!" says Gregory. "I hope we're still in time..." As Rupert holds him up, he hands a folded slip of paper to the astonished town-crier. "Bravo!" cheers someone from the crowd. "Let's hear who the new team are..."

RUPERT AND HIS CHUM JOIN IN

"This team - an unexpected one -
Is led by Dingle...my...my son!"

The town-crier stares in surprise,
Unable to believe his eyes...

The chums get ready. "We'll all play
The same bells we used yesterday..."

"All set?" asks Dingle. "What we'll do
Is play the whole tune two times through!"

"Ladies and Gentlemen!" calls Mr. Jingle. "A late entry for the prize! It's...it's my son, Dingle!" "Jolly good!" says Professor Stave. "Let's hear what the lad and his chums have got for us. The competition is open to everyone, after all..." "This is it!" Dingle whispers to Rupert and Gregory. "All you have to do is follow my lead. We'll play the tune through twice, so that everyone gets a chance to hear it." "A new work!" reads the town-crier. "It's called Nutwood Chimes..."

Leading the chums to the stage, Dingle calmly opens his bag and takes out the odd assortment of bells he has collected. When everything is ready, he turns to Rupert and nods. "Remember what we practised!" he whispers. "On the count of three..." "This is fun!" laughs Gregory as the pals run through the tune. "It sounds even better than it did before." "Keep going!" orders Dingle. "We'll play it once more, from start to finish. A little bit faster this time..."

RUPERT'S PAL WINS A PRIZE

*The audience all clap and cheer -
"Hurrah! The finest tune this year!"*

*"Bravo!" Professor Stave beams. "He
Must have this year's prize! I agree!"*

*The Popton captain brings the prize.
"A set of hand-bells!" Dingle cries.*

*"The Popton team have asked if you
Can join them as a Ringer too…"*

As Dingle and the chums finish playing, the whole audience claps and cheers with delight. "Wonderful!" calls a lady in the front row. "Such a treat!" "Indeed!" beams Professor Stave. "A most impressive composition. Superb improvisation. First rate ringing! Dingle Jingle, I declare you this year's champion…" "Hurrah!" cheers Gregory. "Well done!" calls Rupert. "Well done, too!" laughs Dingle. "I couldn't have done it without your help. You can't ring bells on your own…"

With the audience still cheering, the captain of the Popton team steps forward to present Dingle's prize. "Richly deserved!" he smiles. "I hope you'll play them for many years to come." "A set of bells!" blinks Dingle. "How marvellous. They're just what I need!" "Congratulations again!" says Professor Stave. "I think you'll find the Popton players have something else to offer you too…" "If the lad's father agrees," nods their captain. "We'd be honoured to have him on the team!"

RUPERT SAYS GOODBYE

*"Please," Dingle asks his father. "May
I write tunes for the team to play?"*

*"Of course!" laughs Mr. Jingle. "You
Can join them with my blessing too..."*

*"Goodbye!" calls Dingle. "Thanks again!
I really needed your help then..."*

*The pals reach Nutwood and agree
To put the bells back secretly...*

Rupert and Gregory look on as Dingle tells his father about the Popton team's offer... "A ringer?" he murmurs. "Playing tunes all the time, I suppose?" "Yes," nods Dingle. "What do you say?" "I...I'm delighted!" laughs Mr. Jingle. "The more bells the better! Of course you must join Popton's Pride! You'll soon be Nutchester's Pride too. Fancy my son being a composer! I knew you were up to something but that tune of yours really was a marvellous surprise..."

"Thanks for all your help!" says Dingle as he bids the chums farewell. "We enjoyed ourselves," smiles Gregory. "It was fun playing all those bells." "The bells!" gasps Dingle. "I'll have to go to Nutwood and give them back!" "We can do that," says Rupert. "There's no need for you to come too. Stay here and enjoy the rest of the day." When the pals arrive home, they plan which of the bells to return first. "Farmer Brown's!" says Rupert. "Let's try to do it without being spotted..."

RUPERT RETURNS THE BELLS

The first bell which the chums restore
Is from the flock of sheep they saw...

"We'll put a bigger bell back now -
This one was taken from a cow..."

At last the two pals reach Sam's shack.
It's time to put his ship's bell back...

They hide from view as he comes out -
"Bless me! It's back!" they hear him shout.

Walking out across the fields, Rupert and Gregory soon spot Farmer Brown's sheep, grazing peacefully. "There's their leader!" says Rupert. "I hope she keeps still..." Walking slowly towards the sheep, he produces the tinkling bell, which she seems to recognise at once. "There!" says Gregory. "Restored to its rightful owner..." The next bell to be returned belongs to Farmer Brown's cow, Daisy. "Well done!" says Gregory. "I hope we can find the other owners so easily..."

Working through Dingle's collection, the two chums eventually come to Sam's ship's bell... "Not a sound!" whispers Rupert as they reach the sailor's shack. "The lights are on, so he must be in..." Handing the bell to Gregory, Rupert lifts his chum up to reach. "Nearly there!" says the guinea-pig. As he jumps down the bell gives an unmistakable clang. "Quick!" calls Rupert. "Hide!" The pals watch from the bushes as their friend opens the door. "Bless me!" he blinks. "It's...it's back!"

RUPERT'S TEACHER IS PLEASED

*On Monday, there's just one last bell
Which needs to be put back as well...*

*"What luck! The window's open wide -
I'll just climb up and reach inside..."*

*Soon after Rupert joins his friends
A bell rings and their chatter ends...*

*"A joke's a joke. You've had your fun,
But no more pranks please, everyone!"*

On Monday, Rupert and Gregory hurry to school to return the last of Dingle's bells... "We should just have time!" says Gregory. "Dr. Chimp's already there but I haven't seen anyone else..." As soon as they arrive, Rupert makes his way around the building, towards the headmaster's study. To his delight, he finds the window wide open. Clambering up, he reaches in and puts the bell back in its usual place. "This must be how Dingle got it in the first place!" he smiles.

By the time that Rupert rejoins Gregory, several of the others have arrived in the playground. "Hello!" calls Bill. "I wonder if we've got time for a game of football?" "I don't think so!" says Rupert as a familiar ringing interrupts their play. "Good morning, all!" calls Dr. Chimp. "I'm glad to announce that normal communication is restored! I don't know where the school bell has been, but, now it's back, we'll say no more!" "Just as well!" smiles Rupert. "If only he knew!"

RUPERT
and the Late Start

John Harrold.

RUPERT'S GARDEN IS BARE

Rupert and the Late Start

*The winter's ended, so's the snow,
But Mr. Bear's bulbs just won't grow...*

*"It's very odd! There's still no sign
Of snowdrops in this bed of mine!"*

*"Hello there, Rupert! Are you free
To come out for a walk with me?"*

*"Let's see if Nutwood's shrubs and trees
Are all as stark and bare as these!"*

It is spring in Nutwood. The snow has melted, the weather is milder, but there is still no sign of Mr. Bear's bulbs... "I don't understand it!" he tells Rupert, as he peers at the flower bed. "Everything in the garden is so much later than normal. Crocuses should be out by now and the daffodils and tulips well on their way. We haven't even had any snowdrops yet! I don't know what's gone wrong, but I've never known the garden look so bare. It's as if we were still in January!"

Rupert and his father are still out in the garden when a visitor arrives... "Hello, there!" calls Ottoline. "Are you busy, or would you like to come for a walk?" "We're looking at the bulbs," explains Rupert. "They're very late this year..." "Ours too!" says his chum. "The trees on the common don't seem very far-on either. There should be catkins on the willows by now." "Let's go and see if there are any flowers," says Rupert. The pair set off together to see what they can find...

RUPERT FINDS THAT SPRING IS LATE

*"I've got a feeling something's wrong!
I've never known spring take so long..."*

*"The Imps are who we ought to ask -
Beginning spring each year's their task!"*

*"They live below ground. Let me see -
We need to find a hollow tree..."*

*An owl appears. "Who's there? You two
Just woke me up! This noise won't do..."*

To the pals' surprise, the flowers on the common seem just as late as the ones in Rupert's garden... "It's as bare as winter!" says Ottoline. "The Imps of Spring!" cries Rupert. "That's who we should go and see! They look after all Nutwood's trees and flowers..." "How do we find them?" asks Ottoline. "They live underground," explains Rupert. "You go down some steps inside a hollow tree..." "Where?" asks his friend. "I'm not sure!" admits Rupert. "It's an old oak, with a secret door cut in the trunk..."

No matter how carefully Rupert looks at the nearest trees, he can't see any sign of a hidden door... "Perhaps it's that one?" suggests Ottoline. "It looks as though it's hollow..." Tapping on the trunk, the pair hear a different sound to the others but there is still no door for them to try. "Who's there?" calls a voice. Looking up, Rupert sees Nutwood's Wise Old Owl, blinking in the daylight. "You woke me up, with all that tapping!" he complains. "Whatever are you looking for?"

The owl agrees to help the pair
To find the Imps. "I'll lead you there..."

"This stone shows where you need to go -
The Imps H.Q. is down below..."

The two chums try their best to lift
The rock, but it's too big to shift...

"I don't know what else we can do!"
"Me neither, Rupert! I'm stumped too!"

Rupert explains that he is looking for the Imps' Headquarters. "Why do you want to see them?" asks the owl. When he hears about the late bulbs, he nods in agreement. "It is strange there are none around. Follow me and I'll show you where to go. It's a secret entrance but the Imps won't mind this once..." To Rupert's surprise, the owl doesn't fly to another tree but lands on a large, flat rock in the middle of the clearing. "This is it!" he declares. "Can't tell you how it opens, I'm afraid..."

"I wonder if it lifts up?" says Rupert. He tries pulling at one edge but the rock doesn't move. "Perhaps you have to push?" says Ottoline. To her disappointment, this doesn't work either. "There must be a secret catch!" says Rupert. "Let's try one more time." No matter how hard the chums strain, they can't make any impression on the huge stone. "I wonder if it's locked shut?" says Ottoline as they sit down for a rest. "You might be right," says Rupert. He leans back, only to feel the rock tilt...

RUPERT FINDS THE IMPS' H.Q.

The pals lean back upon the rock,
Then, suddenly, they get a shock...

They both slide down the rock to find
They're in a cavern of some kind...

"A tunnel! Then this must be right -
Look, straight ahead! I see a light!"

At last they reach a little door -
"H.Q.! The place we're looking for..."

"Look out!" calls Rupert but it is too late. Before either of the friends can move, the rock has swung round to reveal a deep pit below. "I'm slipping!" cries Ottoline. "Me too!" gasps Rupert. "Our weight must have tipped the balance..." Sliding backwards down the rock, Rupert and Ottoline tumble into a gloomy cavern, which opens on to a long tunnel. "The owl was right!" says Rupert as they pick themselves up. "This looks like it must be part of the Imps' underground kingdom."

As their eyes get used to the gloom, the pals can see glimmering lamps set in the wall to light the way. "Shall we go on?" asks Rupert. "Yes," says Ottoline. "We should be all right so long as we stay on the main path. "We'll follow the lamps," says Rupert. "They must be here to mark the way..." Rupert and Ottoline follow the tunnel to a flight of steps cut in the rock. "We must be getting near!" says Rupert. Sure enough, the pair soon spot a low door with "H.Q." painted in it...

47

RUPERT MAKES A DISCOVERY

Inside the room, there's no-one there
But maps and charts are everywhere...

On one Imps' chart, Ottoline sees
Her garden marked - with all its trees...

"The dormitory! Let's look to see
If that's where all the Imps can be..."

As Rupert looks inside he blinks -
"The Imps are all asleep!" he thinks.

On the other side of the door, Rupert and Ottoline find a cluttered room full of charts and maps. A blackboard on the wall has a list chalked on it, starting with snowdrops and ending in bluebells. 'This must be where they plan their work!" says Rupert. "I wonder why nobody's here? It looks like it's been abandoned!" Just then, Ottoline notices a chart on the table. "Nutwood Manor!" she cries. "Look, Rupert! This is my garden. The Imps have marked all the trees and shrubs..."

At the back of the room, Rupert spots a doorway which opens on to the Imps' dormitory. "This is where they spend the winter," he tells Ottoline. "All Imps hibernate from autumn to the beginning of spring." Pulling back the heavy curtain, he steps into the darkened room and blinks with surprise... "They're still asleep!" Rupert gasps. "No wonder Nutwood's plants are so late! It looks as though none of the Imps have woken up yet! They've been dozing down here since last year!"

RUPERT FINDS OUT WHAT IS WRONG

"The Imps have been asleep too long!
They haven't stirred yet - something's wrong!"

"Their clock has stopped! Its hands still say
The start of spring is months away..."

"The pendulum's jammed! Come and see -
The clock's been stopped deliberately!"

"Somebody's tried to hold up spring!
But who would think of such a thing?"

Ottoline is amazed to see the Imps all slumbering in their beds. "How long do you suppose they'll stay down here?" she asks. "I don't know," says Rupert. "I've never known them to oversleep like this before. What a thing to happen! If we can't wake the Imps there won't be any flowers in Nutwood at all!" On the wall of the Imps' dormitory is a special alarm clock. Instead of being marked with hours, its face is divided into seasons of the year... "That's wrong!" says Ottoline. "It's still set at winter!"

Rupert goes to look at the Imps' strange clock. As he gets closer, he realises that it is completely silent... "It should be ticking!" he says. "No wonder the bell hasn't rung!" Opening a door at the bottom, Rupert peers in to look at the works. "The pendulum's jammed with a stick!" he gasps. "Somebody must have stopped the clock deliberately!" "Why would anyone want to jam the Imps' clock?" asks Ottoline. "Who can have done such a thing..."

RUPERT SPOTS A SLEEPING TROLL

"It's Raggety! But why's he here?
The Spring Imps wouldn't want him near!"

"Wood-trolls and Imps are enemies -
They think he kills off hollow trees..."

"Let's go and try to wake the King -
He should be told of everything..."

The King won't stir. "It's like a spell -
They won't wake till they hear the bell!"

Rupert is equally mystified, until he suddenly spots a strange figure lying in one of the little beds... "Raggety!" he cries. "Who...who's he?" blinks Ottoline. "A wood-troll!" says Rupert. "He's always up to some sort of mischief! I don't know what he's doing here, but I'm sure the Imps didn't invite him..." Rupert explains that Raggety and the Imps of Spring have always been enemies. "He lives in hollow trees," he tells Ottoline. "The Imps think he kills trees off. Raggety doesn't like the Imps because they cover everything in leaves and flowers..."

Leaving Raggety to slumber on, Rupert goes towards a special bed with an elaborate awning... "The Imps' King!" he tells Ottoline. "We ought to try to wake him straightaway." Although Rupert shakes the sleeping figure, the King shows no sign of waking. "Not time yet!" he murmurs. "Got to wait for spring..." "What now?" signs Rupert. "It's as though they've been enchanted!" "The clock!" says Ottoline. "Let's go and have another look at how it works."

50

RUPERT WAKES THE IMPS

As Ottoline removes the stick
She hears the clock begin to tick...

Then Rupert moves the hand to Spring -
A shrill alarm bell starts to ring...

The Imps are all roused by the bell,
Which wakes their sleeping King as well...

"We've missed the start of spring? But how?
Our clock has never failed, till now!"

When the chums look at the clock more carefully, they find that it is quite easy to remove the twig and free the pendulum... "It's started ticking!" says Ottoline. "Now to set it to the proper time!" says Rupert. Reaching up, he pushes the single hand round, from Winter to Spring. There is a gentle click, a whirring sound from the clock, then the shrill ringing of bells... "It's like a hundred alarm clocks all going off at once!" gasps Rupert. "If that doesn't wake them, nothing will!"

As the clock continues to ring, the Imps start stirring from their slumbers... "Who are you?" they ask drowsily. "Why are you here?" "Rupert?" blinks the King. "Is something wrong? Whatever's happened?" When he hears how the whole dormitory has overslept, the King is horrified. "We've missed the start of spring?" he gasps. "But that's impossible! I wound the clock myself. It's never let us down before. Why didn't it go off at the right time? I don't understand..."

RUPERT SEES RAGGETY STIR

*The King spots Raggety - "Why's he
Asleep here in our dormitory?"*

*The wood-troll sits up in alarm -
"I didn't mean you any harm..."*

*"The winter months are cold for me -
It's freezing in a hollow tree..."*

*"I found a doorway underground
And thought I'd have a look around..."*

As the Imps' King speaks, he suddenly catches sight of a yawning figure in a nearby bed... "Raggety!" he gasps. "He was here when we arrived," says Rupert. "Fast asleep, like everyone else." The wood-troll wakes to find his bed surrounded by angry-looking Imps. "I...I can explain everything!" he gulps. "Comfortable beds these, aren't they? I expect it's easy to oversleep. I didn't mean to stay so long myself. Couldn't resist having forty winks. Hope you don't mind..."

"What are you doing here?" asks the King. "I don't remember asking you to join us..." "No," admits Raggety. "Nobody asked me, I just came across your door while I was looking for somewhere to shelter. At the end of a rabbit burrow, actually. No-one was around, so I tried turning the handle." "You let yourself in?" scowls the king. "Yes," nods the troll. "There didn't seem to be anyone around, so I thought I'd have a look, just to see what it was like."

52

RUPERT HEARS THE TROLL'S TALE

"I found you were asleep in here
And then I had a good idea…"

I stopped the clock, then went to take
A little nap. What a mistake!"

"You selfish troll!" declares the King.
"You nearly ruined Nutwood's spring!"

"I wish I had!" says Raggety.
"It's the worst time of year for me!"

The wood-troll explains what happened when he found the Imps sleeping in their dormitory… "I saw the clock and thought I'd play a trick on you!" he admits. "How peaceful the forest would be if spring never arrived! No chirping birds, no chattering squirrels, no buzzing bees! Just me and the trees…" Raggety sighs. "It would have worked, if only I hadn't decided to have forty winks in one of your spare beds! Far too comfortable for a troll like me! I must have been asleep all winter…"

"Typical!" says the King. "Your selfish prank nearly ruined spring for everyone! If it hadn't been for Rupert, we'd all have slept on until the middle of summer…" "Rupert!" growls Raggety. "He's always wrecking my plans! Nobody cares how I feel. You Imps just do what you want and everyone else has to put up with it…" "Spring must follow winter," shrugs Rupert. "You can't stop the seasons…" "Never mind!" snaps the troll. "I'll be off now, anyway. At least the trees will still be bare!"

RUPERT HELPS THE IMPS

The troll runs off as everyone
Discusses all the harm he's done...

"As you've got so much work to do,
Let Ottoline and me help you!"

The Imps take Rupert to their store -
"This potion makes plants grow once more..."

"We need to spray each plant and tree -
The whole lot, every one you see..."

Darting through a doorway, Raggety runs off along an underground corridor before anyone can stop him... "Good riddance!" says the King. "We don't need to bother about him. It's the late start to spring that worries me! March already and not a bulb above the ground" "I'm sure you'll catch up somehow," says Rupert. "Ottoline and I can help as well!" "That's very kind," says the King. "The more the merrier! We'll make you Honorary Imps. Follow me and I'll show you what to do..."

The Imps take Rupert and Ottoline to a store where bottles of special potion stand ready for the start of spring... "This is always our first task," explains an Imp. "We need to spray all the buds to bring them into flower and all the trees to make them blossom." When each of the Imps is ready, their King gives his orders for the spraying to start. "We'll split into two groups," he declares. "Ottoline can go to the far side of the common with the first, while Rupert stays here with the others."

RUPERT HAS AN IDEA

The Imps work quickly, even so,
There's still a lot of plants to go...

"We'll never manage in a day!
I think I know a better way..."

Rupert runs quickly back to where
The Wise Owl lives. "Good! He's still there!"

"I need your help! Please can you fly
Up to the Clerk? I'll tell you why..."

Rupert follows the Imps across Nutwood Common, spraying the branches of shrubs and trees as he goes... "Well done!" calls their leader. "Make sure you don't miss any daffodils!" Rupert tries to keep up with the Imps but no matter how quickly they go from bush to bush it still seems an impossible task. "There must be a better way of covering the whole common!" he murmurs. All of a sudden, he has a good idea. "Wait here!" he tells the Imps. "I think I know someone who can help you..."

Leaving the Imps to their work, Rupert hurries back across the common to the Wise Old Owl's hollow tree... "Hello," he calls. "I've come to ask your help. It's to do with the late start to spring..." When the owl hears how Raggety tricked the Imps into oversleeping he shakes his head in disapproval. "That wretched troll! He's upset the whole of Nutwood!" "I think I know a way to sort things out," explains Rupert. "It all depends on getting a message to the Clerk of the Weather."

RUPERT SUMMONS HELP

The owl agrees and goes to bring
The Weather Clerk to help start spring...

As Rupert waits, he hears a sound
Then sees a plane as he looks round...

"Hello!" the Clerk calls. "What's wrong here?
Don't tell me you've missed spring this year!"

"It's been delayed! But I know how
We'll help the Imps to catch up now..."

The Clerk, who controls all the weather, from sunshine to showers, lives in a huge meteorological station up above the clouds. The owl happily agrees to take him a message and soon flies off, over the trees and out of sight... "I hope he'll agree to come!" thinks Rupert as he waits for the owl to return. Hearing the sound of an aircraft, he looks up and spots the Clerk's cloud-hopper, following the Wise Owl down to the common. "Hurrah!" he cheers. "I knew he wouldn't let us down!"

"Hello, Rupert!" calls the Clerk as he swoops down to land. "I came as soon as I could. It sounds as if you've got a serious problem with the seasons here in Nutwood..." "We have!" says Rupert. "But I think you're just the person to help us catch up..." The Clerk listens carefully as Rupert explains how the Imps have to spray everything with growing potion. "I see!" he nods. "Sunshine and rain aren't enough on their own! I think you'd better take me to meet the King..."

RUPERT FLIES ABOVE THE CLOUDS

"A rain cloud full of potion would
Reach more plants than your Imps all could…"

The King explains that he's allowed
Six sacks of powder for the cloud…

The Clerk takes off and steers the plane
Towards a cloud that's full of rain…

"I'll hover here, while you let all
The Imps' growth powder gently fall…"

Rupert tells the King how he thinks the Weather Clerk can help. "A special rain cloud is what we need," he says. "A cloud?" blinks the King. "Sprinkled with growing tonic!" explains Rupert. "What a good idea!" smiles the Imps' leader. "Six sacks of powder should be enough to start things going. We normally make enough tonic to keep us busy for a good few weeks…" "Very well!" says the Clerk. "We'll load the sacks aboard then Rupert can sprinkle them on a suitable cloud."

"Good luck!" call the Imps as the Cloud Hopper takes off. Flying high over Nutwood, the Clerk keeps going until he is up above the clouds… "We need one full of rain!" he tells Rupert. "That one looks perfect. Nice and big too!" Slackening speed, he circles over the rain cloud while Rupert tips out the Imps' growing powder. "Meant for Popton, I think!" laughs the Clerk. "I don't suppose they'll miss a drop of rain at this time of year. I can always send them a double ration next week…"

57

RUPERT'S FRIEND TOWS A CLOUD

When Rupert's finished, he sees how
The Clerk will steer the rain cloud now...

The magnet pulls the cloud as they
Fly back to Nutwood straightaway...

"A dark cloud's full!" The Clerk explains.
"It won't be long before it rains!"

The pair fly on until they get
To Nutwood. "Right! All set..."

When Rupert has finished, the Clerk presses a button on the Cloud Hopper's control panel. There is a gentle hum as a mast emerges, with what looks like a small loud-speaker... "A cloud magnet!" smiles the Clerk. "It allows me to steer rain clouds into position. I'll switch it on and you'll see what I mean." Sure enough, the cloud follows the Clerk across the sky, away from Popton and on towards Nutwood. "Better hurry!" he calls. "We don't want it raining in the wrong place."

The cloud seems to grow darker and darker as it follows Rupert and the Clerk across the sky... "It means it's about to rain!" declares Rupert's companion. "White clouds are empty, grey ones half-full and dark clouds like this are absolutely brimming!" The plane speeds on until Rupert can see Nutwood down below, like a model village. "We'll aim for the common!" says the Clerk. "That's where most of the plants seem to be. With a bit of luck, we should catch all the gardens as well..."

RUPERT SHELTERS FROM THE RAIN

"It's starting!" Rupert cries. "Now all
The growing mix we've made will fall..."

The Clerk flies off. "I hope spring comes!"
He calls down to the Nutwood chums...

The pals take shelter with the King.
"Let's hope this is the start of spring..."

"Those primroses didn't take long!"
"The mixture must be extra strong..."

Switching off his special magnet, the Clerk leaves the enormous rain-cloud hovering over Nutwood while he swoops down towards the common... "Just in time!" he laughs. "It will rain itself dry now. A first-rate deluge..." "Thank you!" cries Rupert as he climbs out of the plane and hurries over to join the others. "My pleasure!" calls the Clerk. "I only hope it does the trick!" "I'm sure it will!" beams Ottoline. "The rain should soon reach every plant and shrub in Nutwood."

Sheltering under the branches of a tree, Rupert and Ottoline wait with the King for the downpour to stop. "Rather faster than watering by hand!" he says. "I hope six sacks of powder was enough. We normally mix potion in much smaller quantities..." When the rain finally stops, the chums hurry out to inspect the plants. "Look at the primroses!" cries Ottoline. "Flowering already!" gasps the King. "Perhaps the mix was a bit strong! Never mind, we could do with speeding things up..."

RUPERT'S PLAN WORKS

As trees burst into leaf all round
The pals hear a strange rustling sound...

It's Raggety! "Look what the rain
Did to me! Springtime! What a pain!"

"It serves you right!" declares the King.
"Next time, don't interfere with Spring!"

The Imps agree to help. "This spray
Should stop you flowering straightaway..."

As the growing mixture takes effect, more and more of Nutwood's shrubs and trees burst into leaf... "Wonderful!" laughs Ottoline. "What a display!" While the others look on, Rupert suddenly notices a strangely familiar figure emerging from the woods. "Raggety!" he gasps. "Surprised you still recognise me!" cries the troll, who is covered from head to toe in flowers and blossom. "I don't know how you did it, but you've certainly given the Imps of Spring their revenge!"

"Serves you right!" says the King when he catches sight of Raggety. "If you hadn't delayed the start of spring, none of this would ever have happened." "All right! I'm sorry! I admit I was wrong! I won't ever do it again!" says the troll. "Only, please, please do something to help me..." "Very well," nods the King. "We'll use some of the Autumn Elves' retarding spray. It stops plants growing in winter." An Imp runs off and returns with a glass bottle from the underground stores.

RUPERT SEES RAGGETY RESTORED

*"Hold still!" the Imp calls. "Then you'll see -
The flowers should fade immediately…"*

*"Hurrah!" the troll cheers. "You were right!
They've all gone!" he cries in delight.*

*"Thanks!" says the troll. "Next time you spray,
Make sure there's no-one in the way!"*

*"It's spring at last! I wonder how
The garden looks? Let's find out now…"*

"Are you sure this will work?" asks Raggety as an Imp starts to spray him with the special mixture… "Of course!" calls the King. "But you'll have to stand still!" At first, nothing seems to happen. Then, suddenly, the flowers that cover the stick man start to wither and fade. "They've gone!" he cries. "Thank goodness! I thought I'd never get back to normal!" The troll looks so pleased, that Rupert and Ottoline can't help smiling too. "Perhaps he'll be less grumpy now?" thinks Rupert.

"S'pose I ought to thank you!" scowls the troll. "Though you Imps should really be more careful where you spray your growing tonic…" "Typical!" shrugs the King as Raggety goes back to the woods. "He's forgotten it was all his fault…" "Never mind!" smiles Ottoline. "At least spring's started! That's the main thing, after all!" "You're right!" laughs Rupert. "I wonder how the garden looks?" Waving goodbye to the Imps, the two chums hurry home to see…

RUPERT and

It's summer. Rupert's come to stay
At the seaside, in Rocky Bay…

It is the middle of the summer and Rupert has come on holiday with his family to Rocky Bay… "I'm so glad Algy could join us, this year!" he says. "Me too!" laughs Algy. "I've really been looking forward to playing on the beach." While his parents are busy unpacking, Rupert asks if the two chums can go off and start exploring. "So long as you promise to take care!" says Mrs. Bear. "We'll come down later and meet you on the beach."

the Lost Shell

"Can we go down and see the sea?"
"Of course! We'll join you presently…"

"It's Cap'n Binnacle! Let's go
And join him. You can say hello…"

"Let's go for a walk along the prom," says Algy. As the pals enjoy their stroll, Rupert spots a familiar figure sitting on the sea wall. "It's Cap'n Binnacle!" he cries. "Ahoy, there!" calls the captain. "Good to see you again, Rupert. How would you like a trip around the bay in my glass-bottomed boat?" "It sounds wonderful!" laughs Algy. "Can you really see fish beneath the waves?" "I'll say!" nods the captain. "'Tis like an aquarium down there…"

"Ahoy there, Rupert! Glad you're here!
I've got a brand-new boat this year…"

RUPERT AND ALGY SEE A NEW BOAT

*"Hello, there, Mrs. Bear! Now you
Can hear about my new boat too…"*

*"I'll take these two, if you agree,
And show them what lives in the sea…"*

*The captain leads them to his boat.
"Hop in, and then we'll get afloat…"*

*"Look!" Algy marvels. "I can see
A fish! It swam right under me!"*

Rupert and Algy are still talking to Cap'n Binnacle when Mr. and Mrs. Bear come walking along the prom towards them. "Hello, there!" he calls. "I was just telling the lads about my new boat…" "Glass," says Rupert's mother. "Is that quite safe?" "Absolutely!" laughs the captain. "It's like a giant port hole, that's all." "Can we go for a trip?" asks Rupert excitedly. "Of course!" says Mr. Bear. "Then you can come back here and tell us about everything you see."

Following Cap'n Binnacle to a mooring on the quay, Rupert and Algy find the new boat is a motor launch, with a seat at the back for passengers to enjoy the view… "The glass floor's amazing!" cries Algy. "I can see some little fish already." "There will be lots more when we reach the open sea!" calls the captain. "Lobsters down by the rocks. Starfish too, if you're lucky. Varies from day to day. That's the joy of the sea. Always changing! You never know what you'll find…"

RUPERT'S PAL SPOTS THE MERBOY

The pals peer down, enthralled as they
Head slowly out across the bay...

"A merboy!" Algy blinks. "I saw
Him, looking up at us, I'm sure!"

The Merboy darts behind a rock -
"We must have given him a shock..."

"He lives with Neptune, down below,
Where only sea-creatures can go..."

Rupert and Algy peer delightedly at the fish and swirling seaweed they see beneath the boat as Cap'n Binnacle heads away from the shore and out across the bay. Suddenly, Algy gives a cry of surprise. "There's somebody there. He's got a t...tail, like a mermaid! Look, Rupert. You can see him, staring back up at us from under the water..." "The Merboy!" smiles Rupert. "He looks as startled as you do! I don't suppose he's seen a glass-bottomed boat before."

Recovering from his surprise, the Merboy darts swiftly behind a large rock... "He's one of King Neptune's subjects," explains Rupert as the chums end their tour. "I've met him here before, though he normally keeps well hidden." "King Neptune?" blinks Algy. "The ruler of the sea!" smiles Rupert. "He lives near Rocky Bay too. In a great palace under the waves. There's not much chance of seeing that, I'm afraid. We'll have to make do with seaweed and shells..."

Rupert and the Lost Shell

RUPERT SWIMS UNDERWATER

Next day, the chums decide that they
Should both buy snorkels straightaway…

"What fun, Rupert! Perhaps we'll find
Some treasure that's been left behind!"

The pals peer down at life below -
Enthralled by fish which come and go…

"The Merboy! What's he looking for?
It's something on the ocean floor…"

Next morning, Rupert and Algy decide to explore beneath the waves for themselves. "A face mask and snorkel are what we need!" says Rupert. "And flippers too!" adds Algy. "I can see a pair in the shop window…" In next to no time, the pals have changed into their swimming costumes and are ready to try out their masks. "I wonder if we'll find anything special?" says Algy. "Wouldn't it be marvellous to come across a string of pearls or a gold doubloon!"

Wearing their face masks and flippers, Rupert and Algy find that they can swim through the water more easily than normal, gazing down at shoals of little fish. As Rupert swims on ahead, he suddenly spots a familiar figure, sorting through a tangled clump of seaweed. "The Merboy!" he thinks. "I wonder what he's up to? It almost looks as though he's searching for something. Perhaps Algy's right. There might be sunken treasure here at Rocky Bay, after all!"

RUPERT HEARS THE MERBOY'S TALE

The Merboy can't believe his eyes
And stares at Rupert in surprise...

"I'm looking for a special shell -
It's gold, with precious jewels as well..."

"King Neptune's horn has gone astray -
He lost it here at Rocky Bay..."

"It must have fallen in the sea -
But no-one knows where it can be..."

The Merboy is clearly astonished to see Rupert and Algy swimming underwater. Pointing to the surface, he clambers up on to a rock where the chums can sit too... "You're right that something's gone missing!" he tells Rupert. "I've been searching Rocky Bay for days but there's no sign." "Treasure?" blinks Algy. "Not exactly," shrugs the boy. "But it does belong to the King. He's lost his special trumpet. It's a golden shell, set with precious jewels..."

Listening to the Merboy's story, Rupert and Algy hear how King Neptune rides across the sea in a cockleshell chariot, pulled by two white sea-horses. "He always sounds a special horn to let everyone know he's coming. The trouble is, you can't really hear it underwater. That explains why he nearly collided with a baby whale, who was swimming just off the coast at Rocky Bay. No harm done, luckily, but the King dropped his trumpet overboard and it hasn't been seen since..."

RUPERT JOINS THE SEARCH

*"We'll search the ocean floor for you
And try to find the trumpet too!"*

*The chums dive down and look for signs -
"A shell that looks like gold and shines..."*

*The two friends have searched everywhere
When something odd makes Rupert stare...*

*"The golden trumpet! Can it be?
How strange! It moved away from me!"*

"We can help look for the King's trumpet too!" says Rupert. "Rather!" nods Algy. "I was hoping for a proper treasure hunt..." "Thanks!" smiles the Merboy. "If you two search near the shore, it will leave me free to swim a bit further out. I'll come back in a while and see how you're getting on." The two chums dive down together and start looking for a tell-tale glint of gold. "I do hope we spot it!" thinks Rupert. "Imagine finding King Neptune's special horn..."

Although they enjoy peering at the colourful fish, Rupert and Algy can't see any sign of King Neptune's trumpet. They are about to give up their search when Rupert suddenly spots a strange shell. "It's the right shape," he thinks and dives down for a closer look. To his surprise, the shell moves away as he approaches and disappears behind a rock. Rupert swims round and reaches out a hand. The shell moves again. "How odd!" he thinks. "Neptune's trumpet seems to be alive..."

RUPERT FINDS THE KING'S HORN

*King Neptune's trumpet picks up speed
And heads towards a clump of weed...*

*"I'll catch it!" Algy thinks but then
The shell swerves and escapes again...*

*Rupert dives down to make a catch -
This time the shell has met its match!*

*The chums swim to a rock where they
Can look at their find straightaway...*

Rupert and Algy swim after the jewel-studded shell, which scuttles across the seabed towards a large clump of green weed. Kicking hard with his flippers, Algy speeds forward and makes a snatch at the trumpet. To his surprise, the shell swerves suddenly and slips through his outstretched hands. "Amazing!" blinks Rupert. "It's as if it knew we were here. It won't get away from me so easily though. I'll swim closer, little by little, then try to take it by surprise..."

Keeping a careful eye on his prey, Rupert sinks lower and lower in the water until he can reach out and grab the shell... "Success!" he smiles, swimming quickly up to the surface. The pals find a nearby rock to rest on and examine the golden shell more carefully. "Well done, catching it, Rupert!" calls Algy. "Gave me the slip and no mistake! Odd sort of shell, isn't it? I can see how you'd use it as a trumpet but what made it suddenly move so fast?"

RUPERT SOLVES A MYSTERY

"The trumpet moved! I wonder how?
There must be something in it now!"

"A hermit crab! It's climbed into
The empty shell. That's what they do…"

"The Merboy!" Algy calls. "Hey! We
Have found the trumpet! Come and see…"

"A hermit crab? In Neptune's horn!
It isn't something to be worn…"

"King Neptune's trumpet!" says Rupert as he examines the shell more carefully. "It fell in the sea by accident and was lying on the ocean floor. I wonder? What if we weren't the first to find it? What if someone else had got there first?" "Who?" asks Algy. As he speaks, a small, worried-looking crab peers slowly out of the golden shell. "I thought so!" laughs Rupert. "It's a hermit crab! They're always on the look-out for empty shells. It must have found this one and decided to move in…"

The chums are still looking at the hermit crab when Algy spots the Merboy. "Over here!" he calls, waving urgently. "We've found King Neptune's trumpet…" The Merboy is astonished when he sees what Rupert is holding. "It's certainly His Majesty's golden horn," he stammers. "But what's this? It seems to be…occupied!" "We found him living inside," explains Rupert. "That's what hermit crabs do, isn't it? He must have thought that the shell had been abandoned."

RUPERT VISITS NEPTUNE'S PALACE

"I have to take the King his shell -
You two can come along as well..."

The Merboy quickly leads the pair
To Neptune's underwater lair.

"I've brought two visitors with me
And something that the King must see..."

"This way!" a fish says. "Don't delay -
I'll take you to him straightaway..."

"This is a serious matter!" declares the Merboy gravely. "King Neptune must know what has become of his golden horn. This crab will have to appear before him without delay. You two can come as well, if you want to. You're the main witnesses, after all. I'll lead the way. Just dive in and follow me..." Swimming down to the seabed, Rupert and Algy see a coral palace surrounded by colourful fish and swirling weed. "What a sight!" thinks Rupert.

Swimming through an archway at the base of the castle, the Merboy leads the chums to an underwater cavern where they can remove their masks and breath normally. "Visitors from above!" he calls to a courtier. "We have urgent business with the King!" "His Majesty?" blinks the fish. "I will conduct you to the throne-room at once. I see you have managed to locate the missing horn. The King will be delighted!" "I'm not so sure of that!" says the Merboy.

"My trumpet!" Neptune smiles, "But who
Is this you've brought to see me too?"

"A hermit crab! He found the shell
And wants to live in it as well…"

"You miscreant! How dare you flout
Royal protocol? I'll turn you out!"

"I'm sure he didn't mean to take
Your trumpet…Forgive his mistake."

Following the courtier fish to an inner chamber, Rupert and Algy see King Neptune, seated on a splendid coral throne. "Can it be?" he asks the Merboy. "You have found my trumpet!" "Indeed, Sire!" says the boy. "But I'm afraid it has a new owner…" "A new owner?" gasps the King. "Who is this usurper?" "A hermit crab," explains the Merboy. "Already in residence when the shell was found, I'm afraid. These two Nutwooders can vouch for that…"

King Neptune takes the golden shell from the Merboy and looks closely at the hermit crab. "Steal my trumpet, would you?" he bellows. "Creatures have been banished for less! Even a sand-hopper would recognise this as part of my regalia. Give me one good reason why I shouldn't have you evicted immediately!" "Please, sir!" says Rupert. "Don't be cross. I'm sure he didn't mean any disrespect. Your trumpet is exactly the same shape as a seashell, after all…"

RUPERT WINS AN AWARD

"He found the shell first, I admit!
This crab will be repaid for it…"

"The Trumpet's Tenant you shall be -
And live here at my court, with me!"

The King turns to the fish and tells
It to bring him two silver shells…

"I make you Sea Scouts. Your keen eyes
Are worthy of this special prize!"

"So, you found my trumpet, did you?" Neptune asks the crab. "Full marks for that at least! I seem to remember I offered some sort of reward…" As the crab peers out fearfully, the King's expression changes to a broad smile. "Highly irregular, but I appoint you Tenant of the Trumpet. You will stay at Our court for the rest of your days and serve me as a messenger!" "Hurray!" cheers Rupert. "Congratulate your friend," nods Neptune. "I hereby declare him a servant of the sea…"

Turning from the delighted crab, King Neptune summons his startled courtier and explains that there are more awards to be made… "To the true discoverers of my trumpet!" he declares. "I appoint you both honorary Sea Scouts! A rare award for land dwellers but, by your deeds, you have showed yourselves true friends to my Kingdom." To the chums' amazement, he pins a silver shell to each of their costumes. "T…thank you, Your Majesty!" blinks Rupert.

RUPERT SURPRISES HIS PARENTS

*"Farewell!" the King calls. "You will be
Forever both friends of the sea…"*

*The pals swim back to Rocky Bay
With the Merboy leading the way…*

*"Goodbye!" the Merboy waves. "I'll see
You later on. Just call for me…"*

*The chums run back to show their prize -
"How pretty!" Rupert's mother cries.*

"Enjoy the rest of your holiday, here at Rocky
Bay!" calls the King as Rupert and Algy get ready
to leave with the Merboy. "I'm sure my new
messenger will add his thanks to mine. You two will
always be welcome in Our realm…" "What an
adventure!" thinks Rupert as he and Algy swim
back to the surface after the Merboy. "I'm glad the
King wasn't really cross with the hermit crab. I
suppose he can always find another empty shell to
use as a warning trumpet…"

Following the Merboy back across the bay, Rupert
and Algy soon find themselves at the very beach where
their adventure first began. "Thanks again!" he calls.
"Your service to the King is much appreciated…"
Hurrying back along the shore, the chums show
Rupert's parents the special silver shells they
have brought back. "How pretty!" says Mrs.
Bear. "Did you find those with your masks
and snorkels?" "You could say that," laughs
Rupert. "It's a long story…"

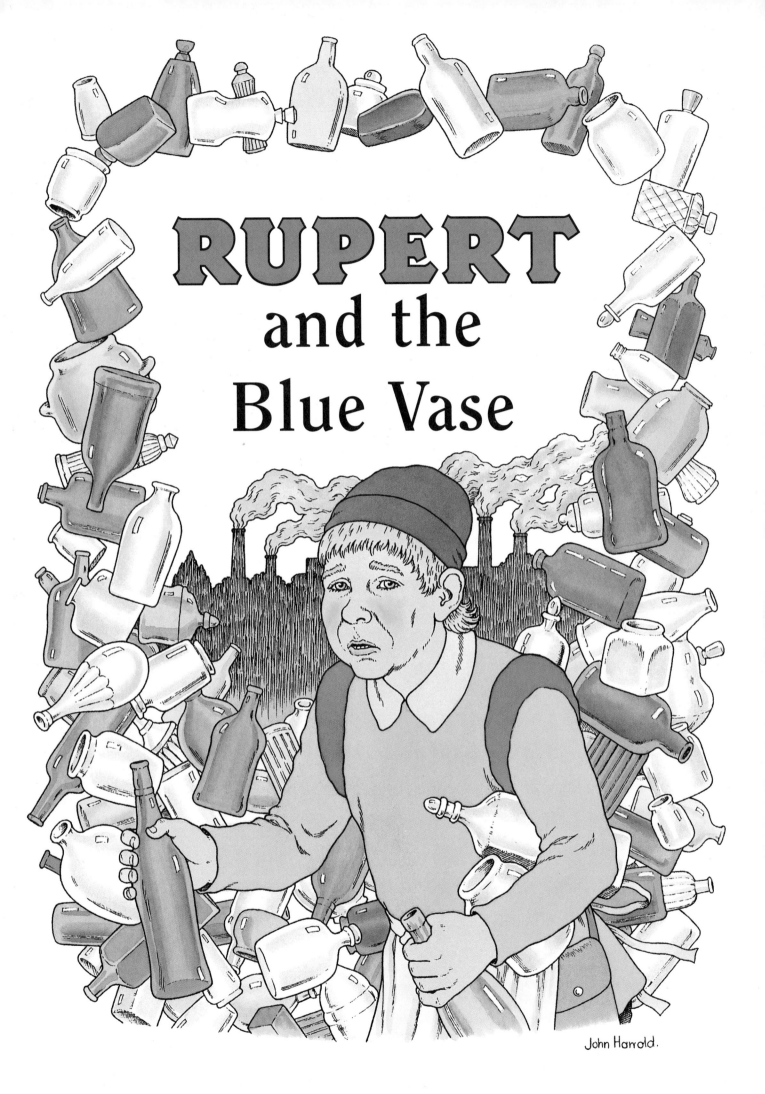

RUPERT
and the
Blue Vase

John Harrold.

Rupert and the Blue Vase

RUPERT LEARNS OF THE BOTTLEMAN

*As Rupert nears the village shop
He thinks his chum's been buying pop...*

*"They're empty!" Podgy laughs. "Don't you
Have jars and bottles to sell too?"*

*"A leaflet said a man would pay
For any that he gets today..."*

*Algy suspects it's all a hoax -
"Another of the Foxes' jokes!"*

It is Saturday morning in Nutwood and Rupert is off to spend his pocket money at Mr. Chimp's shop. As he reaches the high street he sees his pal, Podgy, walking towards him with an armful of lemonade bottles. To Rupert's surprise, they all turn out to be completely empty. "Where are you off to with those?" he asks. "To the crossroads, to meet the Bottleman!" says Podgy. "Haven't you heard? We had a leaflet through our letter-box. He's offering a penny a bottle. It seemed too good to miss..."

Rupert decides to go to see the Bottleman with Podgy. As the pair walk along the lane they see Algy and Bill, who are carrying collections of old jars and bottles... "Hello, there!" calls Bill. "What do you think we'll get for this little lot? A penny a bottle sounds too good to be true!" "It will probably turn out to be a hoax!" shrugs Algy. "Just the sort of thing Freddy and Ferdy would do for a prank!" "I wonder?" murmurs Podgy. "I suppose we'll soon find out!"

*"The Fox twins! Look! They've come to sell
Old bottles to the man as well…"*

*"That's three-pence each!" he smiles. "Well done!
Top prices paid! Tell everyone!"*

*It's Bill's turn first, then Algy's haul -
"I say! Blue glass! The best of all!"*

*"I'll give you two-pence! Blue's so rare
You hardly find it anywhere!"*

When the chums reach the crossroads, they find a horse and wagon waiting there, with a man collecting bottles of all shapes and sizes… "Freddy and Ferdy have beaten us to it!" gasps Podgy. "I wonder how many bottles they managed to sell?" "Three-pence each!" the man declares as he hands the twins their prize. "Tell all your friends to come and see me too! Any old bottles and jars. Top prices paid." "It's true, then!" blinks Rupert. "Who ever would have believed it?"

As Freddy and Ferdy scamper off with their money, the man pays Bill for the bottles in his box. Turning to Algy, he singles out a blue bottle. "A lovely specimen!" he cries. "I'll give you two-pence for that! Blue glass and red glass are rarer than green and brown. I'm always happy to pay extra for those…" "Red glass?" blinks Podgy. "I don't think I've ever seen a red jar or bottle. I've got some red marbles at home. I wonder if they're worth anything? Perhaps I ought to bring them along?"

Rupert and the Blue Vase

RUPERT IS GIVEN AN OLD VASE

"It still seems too good to be true!
I'm off to fetch some bottles too!"

When Rupert reaches home he pleads
For the old bottles that he needs...

"I've no old jars or bottles, dear,
But I think there's some blue glass here..."

"An old blue vase! It's broken now -
I'd mend it, but I don't know how..."

Watching his chums collect their money, Rupert decides to go home and fetch some bottles too. "I'll be straight back!" he calls to Bill. "Old bottles?" blinks Mrs. Bear. "Why would anyone pay a penny each for those? It all sounds very odd to me! Your father keeps old jars for his paintbrushes. I suppose there might be a bottle or two in the cupboard..." "Blue or red glass would be best," says Rupert eagerly. "Blue glass?" murmurs Mrs. Bear. "I think you might just be in luck..."

"I wonder if it's still there?" says Mrs. Bear as she leads the way into the kitchen. Opening a cupboard, she reaches up to the top shelf and takes out a dusty, old vase. "Blue glass!" cries Rupert. "That's right!" his mother smiles. "It's from Venice, I think. We had it as a wedding present. Rather fragile, I'm afraid. It's no use now that the handles are broken. You may as well take it with you. If it was china, I'd have it mended but glass can't really be repaired..."

Rupert and the Blue Vase

RUPERT TALKS TO THE BOTTLEMAN

*"The Bottleman's about to go -
I think you might just catch him though..."*

*"Hello! What's this? Blue glass, I say!
You've brought a vase to throw away..."*

*"A lovely piece! Venetian ware -
Some very fine glass comes from there..."*

*"Although your vase is broken, we
Might fix it somehow. Come with me..."*

Hurrying back along the lane with his mother's old vase, Rupert meets Willie Mouse and Ottoline Otter. "You'd better run if you want to catch the Bottleman!" says Willie. "He's just about to pack up for the day..." To Rupert's relief, the man is still there at the crossroads, sorting the bottles on the back of his wagon. "Hello!" he smiles. "You're the last today, I think. Blue glass, I see! Not a bottle though, from the shape of it..." "No," puffs Rupert. "I've brought an old vase."

"Very nice!" says the Bottleman as he takes Rupert's vase. "Venetian ware, I think. It's a lovely shade of blue." "It was my mother's favourite," nods Rupert. "If only the handles weren't broken..." "I wonder?" murmurs the man. "It can't do any harm to ask, I suppose. Come along with me and we'll see what they say..." "They?" blinks Rupert. "At the glassworks," smiles the man. "About this vase of yours. I can't make any promises but you never know..."

79

RUPERT GOES ON A JOURNEY

The heavy wagon lumbers back
Along a winding forest track…

Then, in the distance, Rupert sees
Some buildings, in amongst the trees.

"Old bottles come from far and wide –
They're sorted here, then stored inside…"

"I've brought a full load back with me
And this vase, for the Chief to see…"

Climbing up on to the wagon, Rupert sits next to the Bottleman as he drives down the lane, away from Nutwood. The heavily-laden wagon lumbers slowly along with a clinking of jars and bottles. After a while, it leaves the main path and turns off along a winding track. "Not far now!" calls the driver. "The factory's just round the corner." As Rupert looks ahead he sees a cluster of redbrick buildings with tall, smoking chimneys. "Always busy!" laughs the man. "Wait till you see inside…"

When he reaches the glassworks the Bottleman drives his cart into a large courtyard outside the main building. A number of other wagons are already there, unloading baskets of bottles. "This is where we make our deliveries," explains Rupert's companion. "The chap over there's come from Nutchester, the young fellow with the foreman has been to Popton, I think…" Climbing down from his wagon, he explains how he has come back with a full load of bottles and a special blue vase…

RUPERT SEES MORE BOTTLES

"I'm glad the Nutwood load is done -
Unlike young Perkins' Popton one!"

"These mixed up bottles just won't do -
He needs to sort them out, like you!"

"Look lively, Perkins! We can't wait
Forever. Get those bottles straight."

"Wait here, Rupert, while I see what
The Chief thinks of this vase you've got…"

"Well done!" says the foreman. "It's a shame all our collectors aren't as reliable as you!" "Perkins?" asks the Bottleman. "A disgrace!" snaps the foreman. "Second time it's happened this week!" The young man from Popton hangs his head in shame. "Unsorted bottles!" says the foreman. "Plenty here but all mixed together. They're no use to us like that!" "None at all!" sighs the Bottleman. "Got to keep our colours clear." "Exactly!" nods the foreman. "It's the first rule of sorting…"

"I'm sorry I mixed up Popton's bottles," says the young collector. "I just forgot about keeping colours separate…" "Well, sort them out now!" says the foreman. "I'll be back later to see how you've done!" "Poor Perkins!" says the Nutwood collector. "It's an easy mistake to make. Did it myself when I was his age…" Leaving Rupert to wait in the courtyard, he tells him he'll take the blue vase to show to the glassworks' chief blower. "He'll know how to fix it, if anyone does…"

RUPERT LENDS A HAND

As Rupert waits, the youth sighs then
Starts taking bottles out again…

"Wait! I'll help you! Together we
Can sort the bottles easily…"

The pair start sorting - one by one -
Until the Popton load is done…

"We've nearly finished - thanks to you!
It's so much faster when there's two!"

Left alone in the courtyard, Rupert watches the young collector unloading the bottles from his wagon. "It will take him ages to sort through that lot!" he thinks. "Perhaps I can give him a hand…" "I wouldn't say no!" smiles the youth as Rupert offers to help. "There are hundreds of bottles here, all mixed up together…" "It will be easy to sort them out if the two of us work together," says Rupert. "Let's empty the baskets first, then put the different colours into groups…"

Carefully unloading the Popton bottles, Rupert and the collector stand them all together in the courtyard. "What a lot!" says the youth. "It's the most I've ever gathered…" "Now we'll start sorting!" says Rupert. "I'll take all the brown bottles while you stick to green…" "Wonderful!" blinks Perkins as the pair refill the baskets. "This is so much faster than doing it all on your own!" "Clear jars and bottles next," calls Rupert. "Then we should be finished, except for anything rare…"

RUPERT HAS A GUIDED TOUR

"Well done, Perkins! I'm glad to see
You've sorted them out properly…"

"What now?" asks Rupert. "Where do your
Old bottles go? What are they for?"

"This way!" says Perkins. "I'll show you
How we turn old glass into new!"

"We gather glass from every town.
Then sort it all and melt it down…"

Rupert and Perkins are so quick at sorting bottles that they have finished them all by the time the foreman comes back to see how things are going… "Well done!" he cries. "We might make a collector of you yet!" "Thanks, Rupert!" beams the youth. "I'd never have managed all that without your help!" "You're welcome!" says Rupert. "What I want is to know why you bother to collect so many old bottles and jars? I thought a glassworks would be more concerned with making new ones…"

"This is a rather special glassworks!" says Perkins. "I'll take you on a guided tour!" Leading the way inside, he shows Rupert where the bottles are taken next. "They're recycled!" he smiles. "Melted down and turned into something new. Much less wasteful than making new glass all the time. Neater too! Nobody normally wants old bottles, but to us they're worth collecting. You'd be amazed at how many we get. Popton's quite small but think of the bottles from a larger town, like Nutchester…"

RUPERT SEES THE GLASSWORKS

"The sorted bottles go through here -
Down chutes marked 'green' or 'brown' or 'clear'…"

"The glass soon melts in this great vat -
The furnaces make sure of that…"

"The furnaces are down below -
Come on! I'll show you where to go!"

As Perkins pushes at the door
It feels much hotter than before…

As Rupert looks round the glassworks he sees two men emptying out a large basket full of green bottles. "One of the most common colours!" says his guide. "Follow me and I'll show you what happens to them next." Walking deeper into the factory, the pair come to a viewing gallery above a second green chute, which tips old bottles into a huge vat of molten glass. "Thirsty work!" says Perkins. "The furnaces down below are kept going all day long…"

From the melting vats, Perkins takes Rupert down a steep flight of steps to see the furnaces… "They're the heart of the whole factory!" he explains. "Without them we wouldn't be able to melt any glass at all." As his companion pushes open a heavy wooden door, Rupert feels a sudden gust of hot air. Red light shines all round and the corridor is filled with the smell of acrid smoke. "Come on!" says the collector. "We won't stay for long but it's well worth having a look…"

Rupert and the Blue Vase

RUPERT FOLLOWS HIS NEW FRIEND

*"These stokers keep the fires alight -
They tend furnaces day and night!"*

*"We'll go back upstairs now and see
The glass-blowers. Just follow me…"*

*The next thing Rupert sees is how
The glass goes to the blowers now…*

*"Each blower dips a rod to take
Glass for the object he will make."*

Inside the room, Rupert sees four or five huge furnaces, with teams of men busily shovelling coal into the flames… "Keeps burning day and night!" says Perkins proudly. "They're under strict instructions to never let the fires burn down. Glass-melting needs constant heat, you see. We can't have the melting vats ever going cool…" "It's certainly hot!" gasps Rupert. "We'll go up now," says his guide. "I'll show you where the molten glass is blown."

Emerging from the heat of the furnaces, Rupert finds himself back at the vats of molten glass. "It flows along a pipe to the blowers," says Perkins. "They're the ones who turn it into something new…" The air is full of steam and smoke as molten glass is delivered to the blowing chamber. "Each blower gathers the glass he needs on the end of a metal rod." explains Perkins. "It's kept warm in a central cauldron. One for each colour. Let's go and see what they're making…"

"It's ready, Rupert! Just watch what
He does now with the glass he's got..."

The glass swells. In no time at all
It turns into a clear, round ball...

"The finished glassware's sent from here
To customers, both far and near."

"Hello, young Rupert! Time to see
The Chief glass-blower, come with me..."

As the pair step forward a glass-blower takes a rod from the fire, with a mass of molten glass. "Watch carefully!" whispers Perkins. Putting the rod to his lips, the old man blows slowly. At first, nothing seems to happen, then, as Rupert looks on, the melted glass swells into a huge bubble. "He'll pinch it into shape now," says Perkins. "They make it look so easy! It actually takes years of training. I'd like to be a blower one day. They've sent me out collecting to learn the ropes..."

From watching the glass-blowers, Perkins takes Rupert to see some of their finished work. "These are all goblets they've just made!" he says. "They're ready now to be packed in boxes and sent to shops all over the world!" he adds proudly. "People are always keen to get our hand-blown glass..." "Quite right too!" calls a voice. Looking round, Rupert sees the Bottleman from Nutwood. "Now Perkins' tour is over, I'll take you to the Chief," he says. "He's ready to make a start on your vase..."

RUPERT HAS GOOD NEWS

"The vase's owner! I hope you
Don't mind if he stays to watch too?"

"A pretty shape! I'll draw in how
The missing handles should look now…"

The Chief blower starts sorting through
Some bottles for a matching blue…

He nears a vat and throws them in -
"Stoke up the fires please! Let's begin!"

Leading the way back through the glassworks, the collector introduces Rupert to the Chief Blower… "So, you're the owner of the blue vase!" he says. "Nice work! Murano, I think. Can I match it? We'll have to wait and see…" Taking the vase to a nearby blackboard, he takes a stick of chalk and makes a careful note of its shape and size. "These are the missing handles!" he smiles, drawing them back in. "It's a little trickier to make them in glass, but I think we can try…"

"Blue glass!" says the Chief Blower. "Not too deep and not too pale…" Sorting through a collection of bottles, he finally produces a pair which exactly match the right shade. "These should do the trick!" he announces. Taking the bottles to one of the melting vats, he throws them in and calls to the stokers to put more coal on the fire. "Hot as you can, please gentlemen! We're trying to match the Venetians!" "He can do it!" whispers Perkins. "Just wait and see if he doesn't!"

*"The blue vase next! I'll melt that too!
Then make another one for you…"*

*"The glass is ready! Now we'll see!"
Rupert looks on excitedly…*

*The Chief starts blowing. Rupert sees
Him make another vase with ease.*

*"It's nearly done! The handles go
On near the very end, you know…"*

As the bottles start to melt in the vat, the Chief Blower takes Rupert's vase and adds it in too. "Gone, but not forgotten!" he calls. "You'll have to trust me, I'm afraid. The whole vase needs making from new. Sticking on new handles would never do!" "Whatever you say," nods Rupert, fascinated by the fiery display. When the whole vat of glass has melted, the Blower takes his rod and flourishes it, like a magic wand. "Now for the moment of truth!" he declares. "We're ready to start…"

Drawing out a mass of molten glass, the Chief raises the rod to his lips and starts to blow. "Bravo!" calls Perkins as a blue ball begins to form. Turning the glass over a flame, the blower pinches it into shape with a pair of metal tongs. In what seems like no time at all he has created a perfect replica of the broken vase. "Still no handles!" he laughs. "They're the last thing to add. There should be just enough molten glass left at the bottom of the vat…"

RUPERT IS GIVEN A NEW VASE

*"Astonishing!" blinks Rupert. "You
Have made the same vase, but brand-new!"*

*"Just let the glass cool, then it's done -
A stand-in for your broken one!"*

*When Rupert thanks the Chief, he smiles.
"I like working in other styles…"*

*"Goodbye!" calls Rupert. "I can't wait
To show Mum her vase. It looks great!"*

Pulling some of the remaining glass into a thin tube, the blower tacks it to the side of the vase then tweaks it into shape. Repeating the process carefully, he finally declares that his work is finished… "Amazing!" blinks Rupert. "It's just like the old one, but brand-new!" "Not bad!" smiles the craftsman. "A slightly different shape to your mother's original but no two hand-made objects are ever identical. That's all part of their charm! Let it cool for a while and then it's yours…"

Rupert is delighted with the new vase. "Don't mention it!" says the Chief blower. "It's good to be set a challenge like that. I wonder if your mother will be able to tell it from the original?" "He'll soon see!" says the Nutwood collector. "It's time we sent him home…" "Thank you for the tour of the glassworks!" says Rupert. "I really enjoyed looking around." "Glad to hear it!" says the Chief as he waves Rupert off. "Perkins is the one to thank for that. Keen young fellow. Should go far…"

RUPERT'S MOTHER IS DELIGHTED

*The pair ride down a winding track -
"There's Nutwood!" Rupert cries. "We're back!"*

*"Goodbye!" he calls. "I'm glad that you
Will soon be a glass-blower too!"*

*"Hello, I'm back, Mum!" Rupert cries.
"I've brought you a special surprise…"*

*"My vase!" gasps Mrs. Bear. "It's new!
But how? Whatever did you do?"*

Trundling along a winding lane, the cart soon leaves the glassworks far behind. "There's Nutwood!" calls Rupert excitedly. "I'll drop you by the edge of the common," says Perkins. "Got to get back in time to help the Chief!" "You mean you won't be collecting any more?" asks Rupert. "No!" smiles the youth. "I'm an apprentice blower now!" "Congratulations!" calls Rupert as he sets off. "Do thank everyone for the vase. I can't wait to see what Mum says when she sees it…"

When he arrives home, Rupert finds his mother is in the garden, hanging out some washing… "Hello!" she says. "You've been gone for a long time. Did the bottle collector take the old vase?" "Yes!" laughs Rupert. "But look what he gave me in exchange…" "I don't believe it!" gasps Mrs. Bear. "It's good as new! However did you manage that?" "I had some help!" smiles Rupert. "But it was thirsty work. I'll tell you everything that happened, over tea…"

These two pictures look identical, but there are ten differences between them. Can you spot them all? *Answers on page 109*

Which Story?

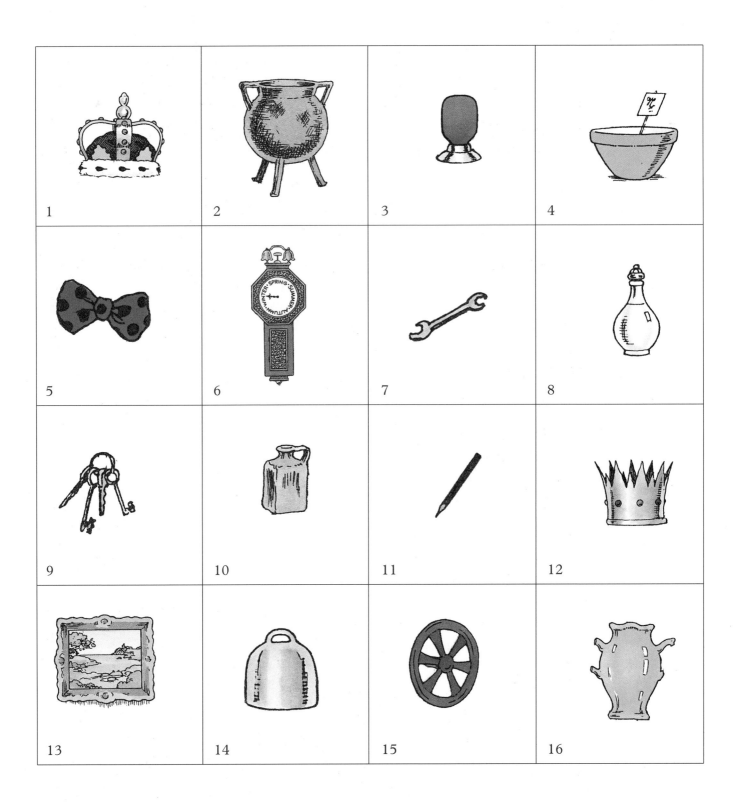

Each of the objects shown above appears in a story from this year's annual.
Can you find out where they are from?

Answers on page 109

Rupert's Crossword Puzzle

See if you can complete this crossword. Most of the answers can be found
in stories from this year's annual . . .

ACROSS

2. Nutwood landowner (6,5)
5. Wet stuff, falls from the sky (5)
6. Large town near Nutwood (10)
8. Take cover, conceal (4)
9. Use again (7)
11. Sleep through winter (9)
12. Turn to ice (6)
13. Rupert's pal from Nutwood Manor (8)
16. Noah built one of these (3)
17. Mislaid (4)
19. Bad-tempered Nutwood troll (7)
21. Knowledgeable castle-dweller, lives near Nutwood (4,3,4)
22. Not empty (4)
24. Appear in 29 Across, care for Nutwood's plants (4)
26. Rupert's greedy chum (5)
29. Second season of the year (6)
32. Type of crab (6)
35. Large expanse of water (4)
36. Small, round cake with currants (3)
37. Nutwood's oldest resident (6,5)
40. Beneath, below (5)
42. Timepiece (5)
43. Controlling official (5)
44. Predicted by barometer (7)
49. Fall (6)
51. Too much 5 across produces this (5)
52. Tired (6)
53. Yellow spring flowers (9)

DOWN

1. Start (5)
3. Glass container (6)
4. Not any (4)
6. Not old (3)
7. Whirlwind (7)
10. Knowing bird (4,3,3,)
12. Last (5)
14. Made by Nutwood's Professor? (9)
15. Not hard (4)
18. Arrangement of notes, melody (4)
20. One of Rupert's chums (4)
23. Not down (2)
25. Mixed-up (8)
27. Shy woodland creature (4)
28. Nutwood's policeman (7)
30. Sound a bell (4)
31. First month of the year (7)
33. Rotate (4)
34. Sea-king (7)
38. Group of sheep (5)
39. Mechanical device (7)
41. Turn snow or ice to 5 Across (4)
45. Rupert's biggest pal (6)
46. Stop (4)
47. Space, chamber (4)
48. Jump (4)
50. Buzzing insect (3)

Answers on page 109

A
P
A
G
E

T
O

C
O
L
O
U
R

How carefully can you colour these two pictures?

RUPERT
and the
White Path

John Harrold.

RUPERT WAITS FOR SNOW

It's cold in Nutwood, even so
There isn't any sign of snow...

"Look, Rupert! Here's the reason why -
The dial says there's none in the sky..."

It seems that Mr. Bear is right -
No snow has fallen in the night...

"There's Bill and Edward! Hey! I say!
I've got a football. Want to play?"

It is January in Nutwood. The weather is freezing cold but there is still no sign of snow... "I wonder what's happened?" says Rupert. "I'm sure we must be due for some soon." "Not according to my barometer!" says Mr. Bear, as the pair come in from the garden. "The dial says 'High'. That normally means a spell of bright sunshine, with hardly any clouds. There'll have to be a change in the weather for snow to fall. Sorry, Rupert, but you won't be needing your toboggan yet..."

Next morning, the weather in Nutwood seems chillier than ever. Rupert gets out of bed and draws open the curtains... "Still no snow!" he sighs. "I suppose Dad's right. We'll just have to wait a few more days." After breakfast, he decides to go to Nutwood common to see if any of his chums want to play football. "Edward and Bill!" he laughs. "They're always keen. All we need is a few of the others and they'll be enough for a match." Calling to his chums, he hurries up to join them.

RUPERT'S PALS THROW SNOWBALLS

"There's Algy, Willie, Gregory...
Perhaps they'll play? Let's go and see!"

"Take that!" laughs Algy. Rupert blinks -
"A snowball! But where from?" he thinks...

"How?" Rupert gasps. "I didn't know
That Nutwood had had any snow..."

"This way!" says Algy. "Follow me!
I'll show you a discovery..."

"A football match would be fun!" agrees Bill. "Let's go and look for the others..." The three friends start out together and soon spot Algy Pug, with Willie Mouse and Gregory Guinea-pig. "Hello!" calls Algy. "Come and see what we've found..." Rupert and Bill start running up the hill, only to be met with a hail of snowballs. "Got you!" laughs Algy. "Good shot!" calls Willie. "Mine missed by miles." "Mine too!" says Gregory. "But I've still got one left. Perhaps I'll have better luck with Bill..."

"Your faces!" laughs Algy as he joins the chums. "We certainly took you by surprise!" "You can say that again!" admits Rupert. "It's not just the ambush though, it's the snow! Wherever did you find it? We haven't had a fall all winter!" "That's where you're wrong!" says Algy. "It's very strange, but there is some snow up here on the common. I found it this morning, when I came out to play. Come on, I'll show you where it is. Then you can all make snowballs too..."

RUPERT FINDS A SNOWY PATH

"Look, Rupert! Here's the snow I found -
A white band, lying on the ground..."

"How odd! I wonder when it fell,
And why it's nowhere else as well?"

Mystified, Rupert leaves his friends,
"I wonder where the white path ends..."

"There's more to this than meets the eye -
Somebody's made a road - but why?"

To Rupert's amazement, Algy leads the way across the common to a wide band of thick, white snow... "This is it!" he declares. "There doesn't seem to be snow anywhere else." "How extraordinary!" blinks Rupert. "It feels as though it must have fallen quite recently." "In the night, perhaps?" says Edward. "When nobody saw. I'm surprised it's not more widespread. A fall as thick as this would normally cover the whole village." "It is strange," admits Algy. "The snow's just like a great white path..."

While the others play in the snow, Rupert and Bill decide to follow the white path and see how far it goes... "It's probably just on the high ground!" says Bill. "The air must be colder up here, I suppose..." To the chums' surprise, the band of snow stretches far ahead, across the fields, as far as they can see. "I can't believe it just fell like this!" says Rupert. "Somebody must have made a snowy path. Perhaps it was Jack Frost, or his sister Jenny, on a visit to Nutwood from the North Pole?"

Rupert and the White Path

RUPERT SEES A NEW MACHINE

"The Professor! Could he be who
The snowy trail is leading to?"

The two chums are amazed to see
A strange machine - what can it be?

"A new invention!" Rupert blinks.
"It's sliding on the snow..." he thinks.

"My snow-mobile! Do come and see!"
The Professor calls eagerly...

Still mystified, Rupert and Bill follow the snowy path away from Nutwood and over the fields. "I wonder where it ends?" says Bill. "The Professor's tower!" says Rupert. "It seems to be leading us there..." As he speaks, the pair suddenly hear a loud droning sound. "Look!" cries Bill. "It's some sort of hovercraft!" "You're right!" blinks Rupert. "It's coming straight towards us! There's a lot of snow swirling around. I hope the driver sees we're here! Perhaps we'd better take cover..."

As the strange craft nears the chums, it suddenly swerves round and slows to a halt. "The Professor!" cries Rupert. "It must be one of his inventions..." "Hello, there!" calls Nutwood's scientist. "What do you think of my snow-mobile? I've just been out for a spin." "Snow-mobile?" blinks Bill. "But I thought they were motorised toboggans..." "Exactly!" nods the Professor. "Only this one's rather special! It makes its own snow as it goes along! Come and have a closer look..."

"So that explains the snow we found!
Your machine left it on the ground…"

"That's how it runs. On paths of snow -
Climb in! I'll show you as we go…"

"The snow-mobile goes anywhere!"
Its proud inventor tells the pair…

He drops the two chums off and then
Drives on, making more snow again…

While the chums gaze at the snow-mobile, the Professor explains that his new machine is responsible for all the snowy paths that have suddenly appeared on Nutwood common. "Much better than waiting!" he smiles. "A freezing spray at the front makes snow, then a giant ski flattens it down. Perfect for cross-country travel! You create your own road as you go…" To the chums' delight, the inventor offers to take them for a ride. "Climb aboard!" he smiles. "You're my first passengers."

Although the Professor's machine is rather noisy, Rupert and Bill are amazed at how fast it speeds across the common. "No friction!" laughs the Professor. "No need to keep to the path either! You can go almost anywhere. It's really the perfect vehicle…" Dropping the pair on the far side of the common, he sets off towards the tower, making another broad, white path as he goes. "What fun!" says Rupert. "And he's left us all this snow to play with too…"

RUPERT AND BILL GO SLEDGING

"Sledging?" blinks Mr. Bear. "But where?"
"We've found some snow! There's plenty there!"

"Hurrah!" cheers Rupert. "This is fun!
The snow path makes a super run!"

Next morning, Rupert wakes to find
It's snowed and left deep drifts behind…

"The thickest snow we've had for years!
Just right to play in!" Rupert cheers.

Hurrying to the garden shed, Rupert and Bill search for a toboggan to take up on to the common… "It hasn't been snowing!" blinks Mr. Bear. "Not here!" laughs Rupert. "But there's plenty around, if you know where to look…" Climbing to the top of the Professor's trail, the pals hop on the sledge and are soon speeding downhill. "Wonderful!" cries Bill. "The weight of the machine has packed all the snow into a really good run! With a bit of luck we can use the Professor's trail wherever he goes…"

Next morning, Rupert is woken by his mother with some unexpected news… "Look out of the window!" she smiles. "Snow!" beams Rupert. "This time it's everywhere!" "There's been a really heavy fall!" says Mrs. Bear. "It's as though the Clerk of the Weather has sent along two lots at once!" "Can I go out and play?" asks Rupert. "After breakfast!" says Mrs. Bear. "But you'd better wear your scarf and a thick coat! We haven't had this much snow in Nutwood for years…"

RUPERT GOES OUT IN THE SNOW

"The snow's tremendous!" Rupert thinks,
Astonished at how deep he sinks…

The road's buried by thick snow too -
So deep that cars just can't get through!

"These snowshoes are the only way
That I can make my rounds today!"

"I want to check that Nutwood's old
Aren't stranded in the freezing cold…"

Rupert hurries out into the snow as soon as he has finished breakfast. At first he is delighted at how deep it is, with his boots leaving huge footprints everywhere he goes… "What a transformation!" he gasps. "It's covered the whole village." As he nears the high street, Rupert sees that the snow is less welcome to Nutwood's drivers, whose cars are unable to get through the heavy drifts. "I wonder what they'll do?" he thinks. "Everything seems to have ground to a halt!"

As Rupert reaches P.C. Growler, he is amazed to find Nutwood's policeman is wearing snowshoes… "They're the only way to get around!" he tells Rupert. "Once you start sinking into the snow, it's too exhausting to go very far." Growler explains that the snow is so deep he is worried about people getting stranded. "It's the elderly and those on the edge of the village who are most at risk!" he says. "Like Mrs. Sheep?" asks Rupert. "Exactly!" nods the policeman. "I'm just off to visit her now…"

RUPERT VISITS THE PROFESSOR

"Hello!" says Mrs. Sheep. "I'll be
All right, if you can shop for me..."

"I think I know a way that I
Can help! At least, it's worth a try..."

"The Old Professor might know how
To help Growler. I'll ask him now..."

"Hello, Professor! Wait for me!
I've had a good idea, you see..."

When Rupert and P.C. Growler reach Mrs. Sheep's house they are relieved to find that she is keeping warm, with a big log fire. "I don't need anything yet," she says. "But I'm a bit worried about going to the shops in all this snow!" "Leave that to me!" says Growler. "I'll be back tomorrow to sort out essential supplies..." As the policeman continues on his way, Rupert suddenly has a good idea. "I think I know a way of speeding up deliveries!" he says. "If it works, it won't take long at all..."

Hurrying as quickly as he can across the snowy common, Rupert heads in the direction of the old Professor's tower... "I hope he's at home," he thinks. As Rupert reaches the tower, he spots his friend, heading for a hangar behind the main building. "Hello, there!" beams the Professor. "I'm just about to have another drive in the snow-mobile..." "I hoped you might!" says Rupert. Can I come too? I've thought of a way you might be able to help P.C. Growler..."

RUPERT'S FRIEND AGREES TO HELP

"I thought your new machine could go
To houses stranded by the snow…

"No problem! It's a perfect test!
First Mrs. Sheep and then the rest…"

Crossing the thick snow, like a sleigh,
The snow-mobile speeds on its way…

"Hello!" says Mrs. Sheep. "How kind!
I need some bread, if you don't mind…"

The Professor listens carefully as Rupert tells him how the snow has cut off Nutwood's outlying houses… "I see!" he says. "And you think the snow-mobile is the best way to reach them?" "That's right!" nods Rupert. "We can find out what they need, then go and collect it from Mr. Chimp's shop." "Splendid!" beams the Professor. "No need to make snow this morning! Perfect conditions for a vehicle on skis. Tell me who you want to visit and I'll take you there in next to no time…"

Skimming over the snow, the Professor's machine crosses the common in a matter of minutes and is soon approaching Mrs. Sheep's cottage… "Back again?" she blinks. "We can fetch your shopping for you!" says Rupert. "No trouble at all!" calls the Professor. "Rupert will write out a list and we'll take it to Mr. Chimp." "How kind!" says Mrs. Sheep. "There are one or two things, if you don't mind…" "Not at all!" says the Professor. "It's good to put the snow-mobile to a real test."

RUPERT MAKES A SHOPPING LIST

The next Nutwooder the pair see
Is old Jarge, digging busily…

"I don't need much, but, if you could,
Some chocolate biscuits would be good!"

Their list complete, the two friends speed
To buy the groceries they need…

"I'm sorry! Nothing's left for you!
My suppliers just can't get through…"

The next person who Rupert and the Professor decide to visit is Gaffer Jarge. He is outdoors when they arrive, digging a pathway through the snow… "Hello!" calls Rupert. "We've come to see if you need anything from the shops!" "Doing the rounds, eh?" says the old man. "In snow like this, you need a sleigh like yours to get through! I don't need much, but more tea would be a kindness. A packet of biscuits too, if you don't mind. Chocolate digestives are my favourites…"

When they have finished visiting the outskirts of the village, the Professor drives the snow-mobile along Nutwood high street to Mr. Chimp's store… "We've brought a long list of things to collect," Rupert tells the shopkeeper. "Sorry!" shrugs Mr. Chimp, pointing to his empty shelves. "I've started running out of stock! No deliveries today, and none tomorrow by the look of it. You're welcome to what's left but I'm afraid it won't go far. Goodness knows what we'll do if the snow lasts long…"

RUPERT HAS A GOOD IDEA

"The roads are blocked by all this snow!
We'll have to wait for it to go…"

"Your snow-mobile might save the day -
If only it could clear the way!"

"Let's see if we can change things round
And suck up snow, to clear the ground…"

"I'll need some wheels, instead of skis -
Perhaps a set with tyres like these…"

"If the roads stay blocked like this, I'll have to close!" Mr. Chimp warns Rupert and the Professor. "It's a serious problem!" nods the inventor. "I wonder if I can come up with some sort of snow plough?" "I've thought of something even better than that!" says Rupert. "What if the snow-mobile ran backwards?" "In reverse?" blinks the Professor. "No!" laughs Rupert. "What if it took snow away, rather than making it?" "Alter the mechanism?" says the Professor. "It's certainly worth a try…"

Speeding back across Nutwood common, the Professor drives straight to his workshop, where the snow-mobile was created… "I'll change the freezing unit first!" he announces. "There's plenty of snow in Nutwood already!" "Will it still run on skis?" asks Rupert. "No!" smiles his friend. "That's the next big change we need to make. Something more suited to grass, I think. There are some spare wheels at the back of the shed. Let's see if we can find a matching pair."

RUPERT TESTS THE NEW MACHINE

At last the new machine's all set -
"Let's try it, Rupert! In you get…"

The pair set off and, where they've been,
They leave a snow-free trail of green…

The new machine works like a dream -
And turns the snow to harmless steam.

"Bless me!" blinks Mr. Chimp. "That's quick!
Your new invention's done the trick!"

After a long spell of tinkering, the old Professor finally declares that the new machine is ready… "It ought to do the trick!" he smiles. "The nozzle at the front will suck up snow, while the new evaporator turns it into harmless clouds of steam!" Reversing out of the hangar, he sets off across the common for a test-drive. "Perfect!" grins Rupert. "We're leaving a green, grassy track behind us!" "Good!" says the Professor. "It shouldn't take long to reach Nutwood, then we can start clearing the road."

Winding their way towards Nutwood, the Professor and Rupert create an instant path through the snow. The new machine is just as good at clearing snow from the road, leaving the high street free of snow all the way to Mr. Chimp's store. "Bless me!" gasps the grocer. "I never dreamt you'd come up with something as quickly as that! It's amazing! Better than a snow-plough and twice as fast. I'll let my suppliers know at once! What marvellous news! We should soon be back to normal…"

RUPERT'S PLAN SAVES THE DAY

The pair drive on, still clearing snow
From roads and pathways as they go…

"Bravo!" cheers Gaffer Jarge. "Well done!
Your new machine's helped everyone!"

In Nutwood, fresh deliveries
Now reach the village store with ease…

"It's thanks to Rupert! His reward
Is all the snow that hasn't thawed!"

After clearing the snow from Nutwood high street, Rupert and the Professor continue on their way to Mrs. Sheep's cottage… "Back already?" she asks. "We've made a path all the way to Mr. Chimp's store!" calls Rupert. "You won't be cut off any longer…" "Well done!" says Gaffer Jarge, when the pair reach his house. "I can normally manage to clear my path, but you two have cleared the whole of Nutwood! Best contraption the Professor's ever made! They ought to have one in every village…"

By the time the Professor has finished clearing the roads of snow, life in Nutwood has already started to return to normal. A delivery van is unloading groceries at Mr. Chimp's store and P.C. Growler is back on duty, directing the traffic… "Congratulations!" he tells the Professor. "You've saved the day!" "It's Rupert you should really thank!" beams the inventor. "I've left him and his chums some snowdrifts up on the common as a special treat!"

Follow Rupert every day

in the Daily Express

John Harrold

ANSWERS TO PUZZLES:

(P.91) SPOT THE DIFFERENCE

1. Cushion missing from Mr. Bear's chair; 2. Pattern missing from Mr. Bear's socks; 3. Stripe missing from Mr. Bear's pullover; 4. Stamp missing from Rupert's letter; 5. Picture missing from wall; 6. Mrs. Bear's broach is missing; 7. Handle missing from cup; 8. Plate missing from table; 9. Hinge missing from cupboard door; 10. Handle missing from door.

(P.92) WHICH STORY?

1) P.60; 2) P.8; 3) P.21; 4) P.105; 5) P.39; 6) P.49; 7) P106; 8) P.9; 9) P.104; 10) P.8; 11) P.32; 12) P.72; 13) P.78; 14) P.34; 15) P.100; 16) P. 78.

(P.93) RUPERT'S CROSSWORD

Across:
2. Farmer Brown; 5. Water; 6. Nutchester; 8. Hide; 9. Recycle; 11. Hibernate; 12. Freeze; 13. Ottoline; 16. Ark; 17. Lost; 19. Raggety; 21. Wise Old Goat; 22. Full; 24. Imps; 26. Podgy; 29. Spring; 32. Hermit; 35. Lake; 36. Bun; 37. Gaffer Jarge; 40. Under; 42. Clock; 43. Clerk; 44. Weather; 49. Tumble; 51. Flood; 52. Sleepy; 53. Daffodils.

Down:
1. Begin; 3. Bottle; 4. None; 6. New; 7. Tornado; 10. Wise Old Owl; 12. Final; 14. Invention; 15. Easy; 18. Tune; 20. Algy; 23. Up; 25. Scrambled; 27. Deer; 28. Growler; 30. Ring; 31. January; 33. Turn; 34. Neptune; 38. Flock; 39. Machine; 41. Melt; 45. Edward; 46. Halt; 47. Room; 48. Leap; 50. Bee.

John Harrold.